PRAISE FOR

Popol Vuh: A Retelling

"In these pages you will find an adroit retelling of a complex and often confusing tale with a vast and bewildering cast of characters. Approaching the *Popol Vuh* with a fresh eye and the necessary erudition, Ilan Stavans, the distinguished scholar of Hispanic culture, nimbly conveys the content and the sense of the original, retaining its magic and fascination while rendering it more accessible to a wider readership. *Popol Vuh: A Retelling* artfully presents the case for the centrality of this magisterial story to the cultural consciousness of the Americas and for the urgency of its message."

HOMERO ARIDJIS, FROM THE FOREWORD

"At a time when so many of us ask ourselves about the end of the world as we know it, few books could be more relevant than this sacred text of the Maya. In a mesmerizing, illuminating new translation, Ilan Stavans brings to contemporary readers this lyrical epic, with its messages from a lost civilization obsessed, as ours should be, with the inevitable cycles of catastrophe and change. The *Popol Vuh* encourages us to contemplate the perpetual conflict between truth and falsehood, light and darkness, so that we may find the wisdom to emerge as better people."

ARIEL DORFMAN, AUTHOR OF *DEATH AND THE MAIDEN*

"*Popol Vuh* is one of the seminal foundational 'texts' of the Americas before it became 'America'—and one so few of us really know much about. Again, Ilan Stavans is infusing the US of A with the cultures and stories that have been traditionally erased or ignored and forgotten. All I can say is, another amazing Stavans project!"

JULIA ALVAREZ, AUTHOR OF *IN THE TIME OF THE BUTTERFLIES*

"The *Popol Vuh* is the great book of creation of the Maya K'iche' culture, and Ilan Stavans has embarked on an intrepid adventure of recreation; he returns to a myth of origin to endow it with vibrant topicality, proving that rewriting a legend is a way of bewitching time."

JUAN VILLORO, AUTHOR OF *GOD IS ROUND*

"Many translators, scholars, and poets have brought us close to the radiant eminence of our Mayan origin story, the *Popol Vuh*. None touch its wondrous dynamism and epic elegance like Stavans and Larios. Free of the formal constraints of the K'iche' original, Stavans's delivers a masterful retelling that invites us into chimeric dreams: from the mischievous first peoples and the quests of those grown from seeds, to hybrid creatures and demi-god twins with battles lost and won. Larios's dexterous admixture of cool washes and vibrant color palettes along with a K'iche'-inspired line-work aesthetic, further unzip our minds to a shared ancestral imaginary. Only my Guatemalan abuelita could cast such storytelling spells over me. Together, Stavans and Larios invite us all to dance as the children we once were and will become. A gift!"

FREDERICK LUIS ALDAMA, AUTHOR OF

LONG STORIES CUT SHORT: FICTION FROM THE BORDERLANDS

Popol Vuh

Popol Vuh

A Retelling by
Ilan Stavans

Illustrations
by Gabriela Larios

RESTLESS BOOKS
BROOKLYN, NEW YORK

First Restless Books hardcover edition October 2020

Hardcover ISBN: 9781632062406
Library of Congress Control Number: 2018956688

This book is made possible by the New York State Council on the Arts with the support of Governor Andrew M. Cuomo and the New York State Legislature.

NEW YORK STATE OF OPPORTUNITY. Council on the Arts

Cover design by Jonathan Yamakami
Cover illustration by Gabriela Larios
Designed and set in Espinosa Nova by Tetragon, London

Printed in Italy

10 9 8 7 6 5 4 3 2

Restless Books, Inc.
232 3rd Street, Suite A101
Brooklyn, NY 11215

www.restlessbooks.org
publisher@restlessbooks.org

To Matthew Glassman and
Francesco Melfi

Contents

Index of Illustrations

CREATION

XIBALBA

SUNRISE

PROMISE

Foreword

ALL WAS A FEATHERED DREAM

The *Popol Vuh* has been referred to by some as the Maya Bible, while the names given to the book by the K'iche' lords have been variously rendered in English as the Book of Council, Book of the Community, Book of the People, The Light That Came from Beside the Sea, Our Place in the Shadows and The Dawn of Life. It is a complex narrative, giving mythical accounts of gods or superhuman beings taking part in transcendent events at an unspecified time in the past, and is replete with details about the natural world, its plants, animals, and environment, explanation of ritual practices and sacrifice, cyclic renewal, and marriage and funerary customs. The tremendous imaginative power of the book gives it credence.

For three millennia, from approximately 1500 BC until the arrival of the Spaniards in AD 1519, the cultures of pre-Columbian Mesoamerica flourished in present-day Mexico, Guatemala, Belize, Honduras, and El Salvador, sharing a 260-day divinatory calendar, religious beliefs and deities, and the practice of sacrificial bloodletting. They also shared the cultivation of maize, beans, squash, and chili peppers, the use of cacao as a currency and a beverage, a ritualized ball game, distinct architectural and artistic styles, and technology. Writing was first used in Mesoamerica by the Olmecs and Zapotecs in 900–400 BC.

Our knowledge of the myths, religion, history, and poetry of the pre-Columbian Mesoamerican civilizations comes principally through the extant pre-Conquest codices, the sixteenth-century texts of central Mexico, and the cosmogonic narrative in the *Popol Vuh.* Much information also comes from carved stone monuments, inscriptions on tombs, stelae, and painted ceramics.

After the conquest of the Aztec Empire by the Spanish in 1521, several missionaries, most notably Fr. Bernardino de Sahagún, sought to preserve the history and language of the Aztecs (or Mexica) by writing down in Latin what they were told by educated native informants. As the first modern ethnographer, in his *General History of the Things of New Spain*, Sahagún recorded the principal aspects of indigenous domestic and public life. He clearly expresses his belief in the humanity of the conquered peoples in the prologue to Book I of the *History:* "It is most certain all these people are our brothers, stemming from the stock of Adam, as we do. They are our neighbors whom we are obliged to love, even as we love ourselves."

The conquerors deemed the suppression of Aztec culture necessary for the conversion of the people to Christianity. Even Sahagún's work was seen as dangerous, and in 1577 King Philip II instructed his representative in Mexico to confiscate all copies of Sahagún's transcriptions, adding that "you are warned absolutely not to allow any person to write concerning the superstitions and ways of life of these Indians in any language, for this is not proper to God's service and to Ours."

Throughout the sixteenth century, temples and images in conquered Mesoamerica were destroyed to root out "idolatry," and hieroglyphic codices were particularly slated for destruction. In his capacity as the Franciscan provincial in the Yucatán, Fr. Diego de Landa oversaw an Inquisition in the city of Mani that culminated on July 11, 1562 with the burning of dozens of Maya codices and thousands of images in an auto-da-fé.

In his *Relación de las cosas de Yucatán* Landa wrote: "These people also make use of certain characters or letters, with which they wrote in their books their ancient matters and their sciences, and by these and by drawings and by certain signs in these drawings they understood their affairs and made others understand and taught them. We found a large number of these books in these characters and, as they contained nothing in which there was not to be seen superstition and lies of the devil, we burned them all, which they regretted to an amazing degree and which caused them great affliction."

Years ago the horror of such devastation inspired me to write this poem:

Archbishop building a fire
with the books of the Mesoamerican Indian
turns the words into smoke

while the painted characters
twist in the flames
as if they were alive.

Archbishop building a fire,
howls.

During the Classic Period (AD 250–900) of Maya civilization, a number of city-states that were also religious centers emerged, first in the forests of Chiapas and the Guatemalan Petén and later on the Yucatán plains. Maya country is found in present-day Chiapas, Tabasco, Campeche, Yucatán and Quintana Roo in Mexico, Guatemala, and parts of Belize, Honduras, and El Salvador. There were invasions by Nahuatl-speaking groups around AD 400, between AD 700 and 900, and by the Aztecs in the Postclassic period. Aztecs first demanded tribute from the K'iche' in 1501, and in 1510 they began paying tribute to Moctezuma in quetzal feathers, gold, gems, cacao beans, and cloth. Moctezuma sent an emissary to the K'iche' in 1512 to warn them about the Spaniards, and they continued to pay tribute until the Aztec Empire fell, in 1521.

A native of Badajoz, Extremadura, Pedro de Alvarado came to know Hernán Cortés in Santo Domingo, on the island of Hispaniola, and joined him for the conquest of Cuba and years later in the conquest of Mexico. While acting as commander of the Spaniards in Tenochtitlan, the capital of the Aztec Empire, he was responsible for the slaughter of Aztec nobility in the patio of the Great Temple during the feast of Toxcatl, held in honor of the supreme deity and god of war Huitzilopochtli, in late May 1520. Indigenous accounts describe the stabbing, spearing, dismembering, and beheading of the celebrants. Three years later, Cortés entrusted him with the conquest of Guatemala, and he set out in December 1523 with some five hundred Spaniards, one hundred and sixty horses, and between seven thousand and ten thousand Mexican allies. He entered Guatemalan territory on February 13, 1524, and made the Kaqchikeles, rivals of the K'iche', his allies, following the tactics of Cortés, whose alliance with Tlaxcalans, Totonacs, and Texcocans had enabled the defeat of the Aztecs.

On March 7, 1524, Pedro de Alvarado and his army seized Kumarkaaj, and the Spaniards subsequently conquered the highland Maya region. The Aztecs had dubbed him Tonatiuh (Nahuatl for "sun"), as his hair and beard were red, and scholars have suggested that his arrival could have been seen as symbolizing the appearance of a new sun, replacing the previous world that had departed.

In one of two letters to Hernán Cortés about the conquest of Guatemala, Pedro de Alvarado wrote: "And seeing that by fire and sword I might bring these people to the service of His Majesty, I determined to burn the chiefs who, at the time that I wanted to burn them, told me, as it will appear in their confessions, that they were the ones who had ordered the war against me and were the ones also who made it. They told me about the way they were to do so, to burn me in the city, and that with this thought (in their minds) they had brought me there, and that they had ordered their vassals not to come and give obedience to our Lord the Emperor, nor help us, nor do anything else that was right. And as I knew them to have such a bad disposition toward the service of His Majesty, and to insure the good and peace of this land, I burnt them, and sent to burn the town and to destroy it, for it is a very strong and dangerous place, that more resembles a robbers' stronghold than a city. . . . And as far as touched the war, I have nothing more at present to relate, but that all the prisoners of war were branded and made slaves, of whom I gave His Majesty's fifth part to the treasurer, Baltasar de Mendoza, which he sold by public auction, so that the payment to His Majesty should be secure."

The apogee of the Maya began toward the fourth century AD. Religion became organized, and the achievements of Mayan art show they were the most gifted scientists and artists of all the Mesoamerican peoples. Highly developed in astronomy and computation, they were also superb painters and stone-carvers.

The Mayan language family is extensive, descending from the Proto-Mayan language believed to have been spoken at least five thousand years ago. At the time of the Conquest, the Maya had an elaborate writing system to record their ancient history. Early in the first millennium AD the Maya developed a hieroglyphic, phonetic script, which they used to record texts and inscriptions on accordion-folded bark paper and deerskin coated with lime plaster, and on finely painted pottery vessels, wood, and reliefs in stucco and stone. Scribes and artists were illustrious members of Maya society.

Only four incomplete pre-Columbian Maya codices—none from the Guatemalan highlands—have survived, but the existence of two great texts written after the Conquest, the *Popol Vuh* and the *Books of Chilam Balam*, written in the seventeenth and eighteenth centuries, are evidence of a rich tradition. Other sources that complement and illustrate these written testimonies include pictorial and hieroglyphic imagery on vases and plates, engraved bones and shells, sculpted stelae, cave paintings, and petroglyphs. Artists and scribes worked with brush and stylus, and even gods are shown painting or carving.

Soon after the arrival of the Spaniards in1524, priests taught the highland Maya nobility to write their language, K'iche', in a form of Latin script, and they transcribed some of their books. Using the Roman alphabet, learned men from lordly families would have written the *Popol Vuh* in K'iche' in the 1550s. Its tripartite narrative of the creation of the world and its first inhabitants, the exploits of gods and heroes, and the history of the highland Maya, is the earliest and most comprehensive document of myths and noble lineages in a language native to the Americas, recording the history of the K'iche' kings until 1550. Scholars believe the *Popol Vuh* derives from a pre-Columbian codex written in Maya hieroglyphics, now lost.

There were three principal K'iche' peoples at the time of the Spanish conquest: the Nima, who were descended from the first four human beings, the Tamub, and the Ilokab. As the *Popol Vuh* was written by members of the Nima K'iche', their ancestry is given prominence. The *Popol Vuh* is history written by the vanquished, though it was saved for posterity by a representative of the victors. Today the K'iche' are the largest ethnic Maya group in Guatemala.

The Dominican friar Francisco Ximénez de Quesada came from Spain to Guatemala in 1688 as a twenty-two-year-old acolyte, learning the Maya highlands languages K'iche' and Kaqchikel while completing his novitiate and beginning his service as a priest. He was transferred to Chichicastenango, a town surrounded by mountains, in 1701, and it was there he discovered the existence of the *Popol Vuh* manuscript. He was able to borrow it from its keepers in order to transcribe the text and translate it into Spanish. The borrowed document has disappeared. After passing through several hands, Father Ximénez's original transcription found a permanent home at the Newberry Library in Chicago in 1911. It is only thanks to his transcription that this literary and spiritual masterpiece is known.

The title page reads, "Here begin the stories of the origin of the Indians of this province of Guatemala translated from the K'iche' language into Castilian for the greater convenience of the ministers of the Evangile." The text follows, in parallel K'iche' and Spanish columns.

—

A foundational creation myth is a fundamental part of every society, culture, and religion, a story that narrates how the world began and came to be inhabited by humans and other species. If the narrative describes the ordering of the cosmos out of chaos, it is also a cosmogony. Creation in the *Popol Vuh* does not happen out of nothing, as sky and water are preexistent.

For me, the *Popol Vuh* is the mythology of nature. Gods, men, trees, and animals all play a part in shaping the Dawn of Life. The events take place in a space and time characterized by mythological and ecological elements, unlike the anthropocentric Genesis of the Old Testament. I have always thought that the gray whale was created in Mexico's Laguna San Ignacio, in Baja California Sur, where the whales mate and give birth to their calves, which would be more consistent with Maya beliefs. The *Popol Vuh* begins with the Maya gods stirring in the darkness of the primordial sea and ends with the splendor of the Maya lords who founded the K'iche' kingdom. Depicted on ceramic vessels, chiseled stelae, and illustrated codices we see the Creator, Seven Macaws, Heart of Heaven, Heart of Earth, the Feathered Serpent, deities in the form of caimans, monkey scribes, dancing armadillos, jaguars, and messenger owls. The lords of the underworld, Xibalba, their skulls and joints devoid of flesh, appear seated on thrones of bones. The first fathers were called the men of maize. From our place in the shadows we see, every day, the Light of the primordial sea. In this dawn of life the earthly paradise was forged, an Eden shared by gods, men, animals, and trees.

THE CREATION OF THE WORLD BY THE ANIMALS
(according to the *Popol Vuh*)

Across an empty darkness,
across unmoving sky,
flashed scarlet macaw—
so day broke: and yellow orioles
with turquoise eyes
began dancing a solo of light

and within a mighty ceiba tree,
the 'mother of birds', appeared
a skinny spider-monkey
his privates dangling—and howler-monkey,
scriving prophesies on the mirror of dawn,
and lunar owl, perched on death's arm.

Caiman lurked on a river bank,
his back marked with celestial stripes,
and sharp-fanged jaguar
pursued the fleeing deer; and eagle,
aloft on clear wings, spied the horizon—
and all was a feathered dream: yellow and green,

then figured from water, clay and wood,
came woman and man:
off-spring of the sun,
children of forest and mountain,
with their eyes they could behold themselves,
their voices named the animals.

Heart of the Sky, Heart of the Sea
Heart of the Earth beat as one,
and all the winged creatures, creatures
of the waters and the land
could be, breathe, love, and cast shade.
And life is re-created every day.

English version by Kathleen Jamie, based on a literal translation from the Spanish by Anne McLean

The *Popol Vuh* narrates five successive attempts at creation: mountains, waterways, and trees appeared first, then animals and birds, who were unable to speak, followed by mud men, who couldn't keep their shape. Next came wooden people, who were soulless and forgetful of the gods, and finally humankind. Analogously, the Aztecs divided their past and future into five consecutive solar periods. According to Aztec mythology, the Fifth Sun, called Nahui-Ollin, which is the Sun of the present era, will be brought to an end by earthquakes, and the tzitzimime, or monsters of twilight, will devour the remains of humankind and take over the world.

Since time immemorial, the daily appearance of the Sun in the firmament (and its replacement by the moon) was seen as the principal element of stability in the life of human beings, a constant in a world of unpredictable events and of changes with or without apparent causes. This helps us to understand the deification of the Sun in so many cultures. Where did the Sun go at night? To the underworld, or to an underground passageway, as in some mythologies? Pre-Colombian civilizations observed and worshipped the celestial bodies, giving events in the sky a preponderant place in their daily life and their destiny.

In *Skywatchers of Ancient Mexico*, Anthony F. Aveni writes that "the sophisticated astronomical and mathematical achievements of the people of ancient Mesoamerica followed logically in the evolutionary development of a civilization which intensely worshipped the heavens and steadfastly associated the phenomena they witnessed in the celestial environment with the course of human affairs." By observing the firmament, the Maya established the most complete and precise calendar of their time. Aveni notes: "For the Maya, a single word, *kin*, signified time, day, and the sun. Its meaning and glyphic form suggest that the art of timekeeping was intimately connected with the practice of astronomy."

Maya religion was polytheistic. It was also animistic in that everything—animals, rivers, plants, rocks, weather phenomena—was alive and in communication with the supernatural. The sacred was pervasive throughout Maya life and rituals were a constant, whether domestic or collective. Agricultural practices were prominent in their myths. To understand the relationship between myth and ritual it's necessary to see if the myth expresses through the narrative what the ritual expresses through action.

In the definitive creation men are made out of yellow and white corn, equating maize with human flesh. Humans are nourished by the Maize God, Jun Junajpu, and in turn they must nourish the cosmos with prayer and sacrificial blood. This included penitential bloodletting or the sacrifice of individual victims in recompense for having received the gift of life. As in most of Mesoamerica, the Maya offered their own blood to the gods, often by pricking a part of their bodies, such as an earlobe, elbow, tongue, or penis, with a sharp maguey or stingray spine, shark's tooth, obsidian blade, or similar object.

The life cycle of maize is a metaphor for life itself. Today, as in pre-Columbian times, harvested seed ears are saved for next year's planting. The maize dies, to be reborn when planted in the earth. Maize (*Zea mays*) arose about nine thousand years ago from domestication of a wild plant called teosinte in the tropical Central Balsas River Valley in southwestern Mexico and spread out from there. New regulations in Guatemala have opened the door to importation of genetically modified organisms (GMO), including maize seeds. Since 2009, multinational corporations have been allowed to cultivate genetically modified corn in Mexico. A law passed in the spring of 2020 affords limited protection for the sixty-four varieties of native corn, requiring labeling of all corn produced and sold in Mexico as "native" or "hybrid." Identified as "hybrid," GMO corn will still be permitted, and one third of corn consumed is imported, much of it GMO. For more than a decade organizations in Mexico have been campaigning under the slogan "Sin Maíz No Hay País" (No Corn, No Country).

The animals mentioned in the *Popol Vuh*, meanwhile, are endemic fauna of Mesoamerica, many now endangered by human activities such as deforestation, devastating development projects, roadbuilding, cattle ranching, mining, destruction of ecosystems and wildlife trafficking. In Mexico, the so-called Mayan Train is planned to hurtle through five southeastern states, wreaking unimaginable harm on innumerable species of flora and fauna. More than two thousand jaguars—half of Mexico's jaguar population—will be endangered by the project.

The *Popol Vuh* bestiary features the white-lipped peccary, puma, coatimundi, white-tailed deer, and cottontail rabbit (creatures whose tails are short ever since the Hero Twins grabbed them and broke them off), bat (one of which cut off Junajpu's head in the House of Bats in Xibalba), hyena, rattlesnake and pit viper, toad, hawk, and more. Jun B'atz' (One Monkey) and Jun Ch'owem (One Artisan), the twin half-brothers of Junajpu and Ixb'alanke, are the Monkey Scribes, patrons of writing, the visual arts, singers, and flutists. *B'atz* is the word for spider monkey in various Mayan languages, while *chuen* was Yucatec Mayan for howler monkey, and also means artisan. There were no beasts of burden.

In the *Popol Vuh,* the names of three of the first four humans created include *Balam*, the word for jaguar. The Hero Twins saved themselves in *Balami-ha*, the House of Jaguars in Xibalba, by throwing the animals bones to gnaw. When the progenitors sacrificed men, bloodying the road and displaying the heads, they blamed it on jaguars.

A crepuscular and sharp-sighted hunter, the jaguar (*Panthera onca*) is the most fearsome predator in Mesoamerica. At the top of the carnivore food chain, jaguars are at home in dense rain and cloud forests, rivers, swamps, mountains, and caves. Revered among the Maya as a symbol of darkness and the underworld, the jaguar features prominently in sculptures, stelae, figurines, ceramics, codices, and murals, and temples were built in its honor. The Jaguar God of Xibalba was identified with the nighttime passage of the sun through the underworld. The spots on its fur were seen as a representation of the constellations. Jaguars were important shamanic creatures. Symbolizing the power of Maya rulers, they were often the *nahuales*—or animal doubles—of kings.

Today the principal threats to the jaguar are habitat destruction, overhunting of its prey, conflict with livestock farmers, and the wildlife trade. The black market poses one of the biggest dangers jaguars face in Mexico and Central and South America. Jaguar teeth are turned into jewelry, their pelts become clothing and rugs, and their bones are used in traditional Chinese medicine.

Birds mentioned in the *Popol Vuh* include the hawk, raven, turkey buzzard, eagle, and parakeet. King Q'uq'umatz is the namesake of Q'uq'umatz the Maker, Q'uq'umatz meaning quetzal serpent. The resplendent quetzal is Guatemala's national bird, and the male grows brilliant blue-green tail feathers up to three feet long. Overweening pride in his beautiful scarlet plumage brings Seven Macaws, the god Wuqub' K'aqix, to his downfall. Owls are the messengers of the lords of Xibalba and are released from the underworld for helping Princess Ixkik' escape death.

A ritual ball game was played in many cities in Mesoamerica since the middle of the second millennium BC. Using their upper arms, hips, and thighs, the players bounced a rubber ball off the walls of a ballcourt, aiming to get it through stone rings on the walls. Use of hands was forbidden, and the players wore padding. The losers were often sacrificed. Some scholars view the ball game as a metaphor for battle and an enactment of the conflict between good and evil.

The ball game is crucial to events in the *Popol Vuh*. The twin brothers Jun Junajpu and Wuqub' Junajpu played ball noisily every day, and were summoned to Xibalba by the lords of the underworld, who coveted their ball game equipment. After being tricked by the lords they were sacrificed and buried and Jun Junajpu's head was hung in a tree.

The skull spat into the hand of a daughter of one of the lords, and she made her way out of the underworld and gave birth to the Hero Twins,

Junajpu and Ixb'alanke. With the help of a rat, they retrieved the rubber ball and other ball game equipment that their father and uncle had hidden and became skilled ballplayers. Once again the lords of Xibalba heard playing on the court, and summoned Junajpu and Ixb'alanke. After a bat bit off Junajpu's head, which the lords hung on the ballcourt, Ixb'alanke recovered it and replaced it with a squash, outwitting the lords in the ball game. Thus this particular ball game became a metaphor for life, death, and resurrection.

The ancient Maya considered caves and cenotes to be openings to the underworld.

In PostClassic times rulers were thought to have been born in and emerged from caves. At Kumarkaaj a cave with seven chambers dug beneath the main plaza embodied the site of the high god's granting the right to rule to the K'iche' kings. King Q'uq'umatz, the greatest leader in the history of the K'iche' empire, ruled at Kumarkaaj between *ca.* 1400 and 1425 and was reputed to have descended to the underworld, exemplifying the relation between kingship and supernatural forces.

With its enormous pyramids of the Sun and the Moon and its Temple of Quetzalcóatl, Teotihuacán was one of the largest cities in the world and center of a regional empire roughly from AD 150 to 650. The Nahuatl name the Mexica gave to the city centuries after it was abandoned and fell into ruin has been translated as "place where one may become a god."

The gods met at Teotihuacán to create the world of the fifth sun. After fasting and bloodletting, two of the gods threw themselves into a bonfire and became the Sun and the Moon, but when they remained unmoving in the sky the other gods sacrificed themselves to set the celestial bodies in motion. Henceforth, to keep the universe from standing still it was necessary for humans to constantly nourish it with blood, thus imitating and sharing in the divinity of the gods.

Construction of the artificial cave under the Pyramid of the Sun and of the Pyramid itself began in the mid-first century AD and continued for approximately two hundred years. Mexican archaeologists discovered the cave by chance in 1971. In 2004, I walked and crawled through a snaking 330-foot-long tunnel to a large four-chambered space directly beneath the summit of the pyramid. In the cave, known as the Four-Petaled Flower, scientists from the National Autonomous University of Mexico were doing research to confirm speculation that this cave was meant to symbolize the place where the fifth sun came into being, the cosmic womb.

The principle of opposites was basic in Mesoamerica. Pairings include male/female, life/death, day/night, sun/moon, sky/earth, fire/water. Duality is recurrent in the *Popol Vuh*. Among the godly pairs are Ixmukane and Ixpiyakok, the Grandmother of Dawn and Grandfather of Day; The Creator and Maker, also known as Tepew and Q'uq'umatz; the great ballplayers Jun Junajpu and Wuqub' Junajpu, twin sons of Ixpiyakok and Ixmukane;

Junajpu and Ixb'alanke, the Hero Twins, tricksters who are the demigod sons of Jun Junajpu and Princess Ixkik', daughter of a lord of Xibalba; Jun B'atz' and Jun Ch'owem, the treacherous twins of Jun Junajpu and Ixbaquiyalo, turned into spider monkeys by their younger half-brothers to join the descendants of the soulless wooden people in the forest; Sipakna and Kab'raqan, the conceited sons of boastful Wuqub' K'aqix/Seven Macaws and Chimalmat.

The Lords of Death of Xibalba also come in pairs: Jun Kame and Ququb' Kame; Xixiripat and Kuchumakik; Ajalpuj and Ajalkana'; Chamiyab'aq and Chamiyajom; Ajalmes and Ajaltoqt'ob; Kik'xik and Patan.

And many of the K'iche' people mentioned in the *Popol Vuh* are siblings, such as Kokawib and Kokabib, or kingly pairs, such as Quicab and Cavizimah.

The Maya believed that the sky is held up by trees of different species and colors: red in the east, where the sun is born, white in the north, whence come winter rains, black in the west, where the sun dies, yellow in the south, the great side of the sun, with a mighty green tree, the ceiba, in the center. The ceiba is the World Tree, its branches in the heavens, its trunk on Earth, its roots in the Underworld. If we cut down the ceiba, the firmament will collapse upon us.

In these pages you will find an adroit retelling of a complex and often confusing tale with a vast and bewildering cast of characters. Approaching the *Popol Vuh* with a fresh eye and the necessary erudition, Ilan Stavans, the distinguished scholar of Hispanic culture, nimbly conveys the content and the sense of the original, retaining its magic and fascination while rendering it more accessible to a wider readership. *Popol Vuh: A Retelling* artfully presents the case for the centrality of this magisterial story to the cultural consciousness of the Americas and for the urgency of its message.

—HOMERO ARIDJIS, WITH BETTY FERBER

Characters

◆ THE DEITIES ◆

Heart of Heaven, Heart of Earth, poetic name of God

Juraqan, whose power shakes nature, **Chipi-Kakulha**, and **Raxa-Kakulha**, who together comprise Heart of Heaven, Heart of Earth

Ixmukane and **Ixpiyakok**, Grandmother of Dawn and Grandfather of Day

The Creator and Maker, also known as **Tepew** and **Q'uq'umatz**

Jun Junajpu and **Wuqub' Junajpu**, twin sons of Ixmukane and Ixpiyakok

Junajpu and **Ixb'alanke**, hero twins, demigod sons of Jun Junajpu and Ixkik'

Jun B'atz' and **Jun Ch'owem**, who make music, older sons of Jun Junajpu and Ixbaquiyalo

Ixbaquiyalo, bearer of monkeys

Princess Ixkik', daughter of Kuchumakik, a lord of Xibalba

Wuqub' K'aqix, known as Seven Macaws

Chimalmat, wife of Seven Macaws

Sipakna, shrewd, calculating, and resourceful, and **Kab'raqan**, who resembles an earthquake, children of Wuqub' K'aqix and Chimalmat

• THE LORDS OF XIBALBA •

Jun Kame and **Ququb' Kame**, supreme lawmakers of Xibalba

Xixiripat and **Kuchumakik**, who cause people to vomit

Ajalpuj and **Ajalkana'**, who make pus ooze from the skin of the legs and face

Chamiyab'aq and **Chamiyajom**, sheriffs of Xibalba, who make people into *calaveras*

Ajalmes and **Ajaltoqt'ob**, who cause heart attacks

Kik'xik and **Patan**, who provoke road accidents

• THE K'ICHE' PEOPLE •

Balam Kitze, **Balam Aqab**, **Majukutaj**, and **Iq Balam**: first humans to be created

Kaja Paluna, **Chomija**, **Tzununija**, and **Kaquixaja**: their four wives

Ixtah and **Ixpuch**, maiden daughters of noblemen

Kokawib and **Kokabib**, sons of Balam Kitze

Kuakul and **Koakutek**, sons of Balam Aqab

Kuajaw, son of Majukutaj

Nakxit, King of the East

Konake and **Belejeb Queh**, of the fourth generation of kings

King Kotuja and **Iztayul**, also known as **Ahpop** and **Ahpop Kamja**, who reigned in the beautiful city called Izmaki

King Q'uq'umatz, of the fifth generation of humans, greatest leader the K'iche' nation has ever known

Quicab and **Cavizimah**, two great kings prophesized by King Q'uq'umatz

Kikab and **Kavizimaj**, twin girls who tell Father Ximénez the *Popol Vuh*

Xulu and **Pakam**, seers

✦ OTHER IDOLS ✦

Tojil, which means payment, debt, obligation, or tribute, but also thunder

Awilix, who sometimes appears as a young man

Jakavitz, forming a quartet with Tojil, Awilix, and Nikatakaj

Nikatakaj, fourth component of the idol quartet

✦ THE WHITE MEN ✦

Father Francisco Ximénez, healer who lived among the white, bearded men. He writes down the *Popol Vuh* in Castilian

◆ THE ANIMALS ◆

Xekotkowach, turkey buzzard

Camazotz, vampire bat

Kotzbalam, jaguar

Tukumbalam, puma

Tamazul, toad

Sakikas, snake

Lotz'kik, hawk

Ixtzul, centipede

Chitic, armadillo

Yak, fox

Utiw, coyote

Kel, parakeet

EMPIEZAN LAS HIS
TORIAS DEL ORIGEN DE LOS INDIOS DE
ESTA PROVINÇIA DE GVATEMALA
TRADVZIDO DE LA LENGVA QVI-
CHE EN LA CASTELLANA PA-
RA MAS COMMODIDAD DE
LOS MINISTROS DE EL
Sto EVANGELIO

POR EL R.P.F. FRANZIS
CO XIMENEZ CV
RA DOCTRINERO POR EL REAL PATRO-
NATO DEL PVEBLO DE Sto THOMAS CHVILA.

Cap. 1. de el ser de Dios.

ARE V XE OHER
tzih varal Quiche vbi.

1 Varal xchicatzibah vi xchica-
tiquiba vi oher tzih, vticaribal,
vxenabal puch ronohel xban,
pa tinamit quiche, ramac quiche vinac; are cut xchicacam
vi vcutunizaxic, vcalahobiza-
xic, vtzihoxic puch euaxibal
zaquiribal rumal tzacol bitol
alom, qaholom quibi hunahpu vuch, hun ahpu vtiu, zaquinima tziis, tepeu gucumatz
vqux cho, vqux palo, ahra-
xalac, ah raxa tzel chuqhaxic, rachbixic, rach tzihoxic
ri iyom, mamom xpiyacoc,
xmucane vbi, matzanel chu-
qenel camul iyom, camul
mamom chuqhaxic pa quiche
2 tzih. ta xquitzihoh ronohel
ruq xquiban chic chi zaquil
qolem, zaquil tzih. vae xchicatzibah chupan chic vtzih-
bal Dios pa christianoil chic
xchiqaelezah rumal maha-
bi chic ilbal re popo vuh. ilbal zac petenac chaca palo.
vtzihoxic camuhibal ilbal za-
qalem chuqhaxic. qo nabe
vuhi, za hoher tzibam puch, za-
eual vuach ilol re, bizol re,
nim vpeoxic, vtzihoxic puch,
3 ta chiqhiz tzuk ronohel cah
gener. cap. 8. vleu, vcah tzucuxic, vcah
xucutaxic retaxic, vcah
cheexic, vmeh camaxic, vyuc-
camaxic vparuch, vpa vleu
cah tzuc, cah xucut chuqhaxic rumal ri tzacol bitol
vchuch, vqahau qazlem vi-
naquirem, abanel, guxla-
nel, alay rech, guxlay-
rech zaquil amaquil, za-
quil al, zaquil qahol, ah-
biz, ahnaoh chirech ronohel

ESTE ES EL PRINCIPIO DE LAS
antiguas historias aqui en el quiche.

Aqui escriviremos, y empezaremos las
antiguas historias, su principio, y comien-
zo de todo lo que fue hecho en el pueblo de
el quiche, su pueblo de los indios quichees;
y de aqui tomaremos su ser declarado, y
manifestado, y su ser relatado, la esconde-
dura, y aclaradura, por el formador, y criador madre, y Padre que asi se llaman, hunahpu vuch. hun ahpu vtiu. zaquinima tziis
tepeu. gucumatz. vquxcho. vquxpalo (ver-
bos, e atributos. que significan vn tirador, tacua-
ajin. vn tirador coyote. blanco pizote. Sor
fuerte culebra. corazon de la laguna. corazon de el mar.) el de el verde cajete, el
de la verde xicara son llamados. y junta-
mente es dicho, y hablado de aquella abuela, y abuelo que se llamaban: xpiyacoc, y
xmucane. nombres propios. amparado-
res, y encubridores dos veses abuela, y dos
veses abuelo son dichos en las historias quichees. que comunicaron todo con lo que hi-
cieron despues en el estado de la claridad
y en la palabra de claridad. esto escri-
uiremos ya en la ley de Dios, en la cris-
tiandad, lo sacaremos porque ya no ay libro comun, original donde verlo. de la
otra parte de el mar es venido donde se o-
cultó, y es dicho su ser enseñado nuestra
obscuridad con la miradura de la clara
vida. antiguamente auia libro original
que se escriuio antiguamente; sino que esta escondido al que lo mira, y al que lo piensa.
grande es su venida, y su ser enseñado.
que se acabo de formar todo el cielo, y la tierra, su ser cuadrado, su ser repartido
en cuatro partes, su ser señalado, su ser
amojonado en cuatro partes, su ser medido a
mecates, o cuerdas, y su ser estirada la
cuerda en el cielo, y en la tierra, y es dicho de cuatro esquinas, y cuatro lados
por el formador, y criador. su madre y su Pe.
de la vida. y de la creacion. que da respira-
cion, y resuello, paridor, y cuidador, de
la paz, claridad de los hijos, ponderador, y cor-

Popol Vuh

Man ixtzaq pa le qajib'al
Je ri' pa le paqalik re le b'e.
Man kiraq ri k'axk'olil,
man chikij man chi kiwach,
man jun sutaq ke'ixuq'osij.
Yab'a chike utzilaj taq b'e,
Je'lalaj taq kolom b'e.

Que no caigan en la bajada,
ni en la subida del camino.
Que no encuentren obstáculos,
ni detrás ni delante de ellos,
ni cosa que los golpee.
Concédeles buenos caminos,
hermosos caminos planos.

Let them not stumble on the descent,
nor as they ascend the path.
Let them not encounter hurdles,
neither behind nor in front of them,
nor anything that hurts them.
Allow them fine paths,
beautiful, even roads.

—POPOL VUH

Overture

Sunset has fallen on the K'iche' people. Our lands have been taken away, our leaders have been subjugated, our children have been stolen. We've been forced to migrate. Our voice has been silenced.

I tell these stories of the ancient world (*ojer tizj*) to once again ignite our people's hearts. My mother told them to me, she got them from her own mother, and so on. They explain how nature is ruled by opposites: truth and lies, light and darkness, sound and silence. Humans swing on a pendulum without ever becoming static.

Heart of Heaven, Heart of Earth, which is the poetic name of God, first made the world out of nothing, then designed the animal kingdom. Since no creature could honor creation, wooden people were made. But they could not speak; nor did they have insight. The Creator and Maker decided to rehearse with humans, although several failed attempts were made in this regard as well. Maybe we, humans, are also only an experiment.

Too much pride and anger. A better version of ourselves might one day emerge.

There is an above and a below in creation. The below is called Xibalba. It's a labyrinthine city with its own rules. The tribulations of the hero twins, the demigods Junajpu and Ixb'alanke, map all that is beautiful in the natural world and ominous in Xibalba.

Passed on by generations, these stories depend on us, the K'iche' people in captivity. They originated with our ancestors, whose names are Ixmukane and Ixpiyakok, Grandmother of Dawn and Grandfather of Day. We are currently under a new law of God and Christianity, dismayed that our faces are hidden and the *Popol Vuh*, the book of the woven mat, is no longer heard.

I speak to you, Ixtah and Ixpuch, so your magic will be implemented again, as it was in yesteryear. It is essential that these stories fall into just the right ears. It's wrong to believe I have concealed this work to avoid retaliation from the bearded white men. On the contrary, our predecessors were encouraged by friars. They even recited these stories under the friars' supervision. The friar Bartolomé de Las Casas, known as the "Defender of Indigenous People," was familiar with our practices. He discusses them in his work *Apologetica Historia Sumaria*.

Having traveled orally, our stories were faithfully written down in the K'iche' language, using a Latin script introduced by Dominican and Franciscan friars, in Santa Cruz, near the ruins of Cumarcah, Guatemala, in the years between 1554 and 1558, with Juan de Rojas and Juan Cortés as rulers, in order to unify our people, to grant them a sense of purpose and build a path of resistance, since nations without memory have no chance on this earth.

Yet, as displacement has befallen the K'iche' people, who have been dispersed in hundreds of diasporas, they have forgotten the learnings of the *Popol Vuh*. Not all our myths are ciphered in this book. For instance, in the work called *Título de Totonicapán* the sun is portrayed as a young man named Hunahpu and the moon as a young woman by the name of Xbalanque. The *Popol Vuh* makes no distinction among genders. We also derive some ideas from Mexican myths.

May we find the strength again to bring it back. May we become *qas winaq*, true maize-eating persons.

Part I: Creation

1

In the beginning, everything is placid. The womb of the sky is empty. Everything is still. Time has not yet begun. There are no humans. Nor is there bird, fish, crab, tree, stone, hollow, canyon, meadow, or forest. Only the sky exists, as well as water, which is in repose.

Earth has not manifested itself. Nothing moves or makes a sound. It is the dark night. The Creator and Maker, Tepew and Q'uq'umatz, are in the water, surrounded by clarity. They are hidden behind green feathers. They are supported by the omnipotent Heart of Heaven, Heart of Earth.

Q'uq'umatz, a plumed serpent with quetzal feathers, is in conversation with Tepew. They decide that, when dawn arrives, humans shall be created. First, they plan the birth of life. That is how it is agreed with Heart of Heaven, Heart of Earth.

Tepew and Q'uq'umatz go on conferring. They discuss life: creating light, how dawn will arrive, who will produce food. "Let it be! There is no darkness without light, no sound without silence. The womb of the sky shall be filled! Let water recede, emptying space! Let Earth emerge and dawn come to Heaven and Earth! Time must begin its course; otherwise there is no memory. There shall be no glory in our creation until humans are made. They will be the ones to remember."

Earth is thus created. It happens by multiple starts and restarts, by trial and tribulation. The Creator and Maker, the guardians of language, declare: "This is how Earth is shaped. Creation is like fog, like a cloud of dust. Water gives way to mountains, which manifest their *nawal*, their spirit essence. Mountains reach higher. They are followed by the emergence of cypresses and pine trees covering the face of the earth."

Joyfully, Q'uq'umatz says: "Your blessings have been kind, Heart of Heaven, Heart of Earth. You are made of three: Juraqan, whose power shakes nature, Chipi-Kakulha, and Raxa-Kakulha."

The three respond: "Our work is done."

The valleys are then formed. As time begins, waterways soon find their paths. There is no stopping change now. Everything is in constant movement. Trees populate the mountains. Perfection is achieved: thought is followed by dialogue and crowned by execution.

2

Animals are conceived. They are the guardians of the forest, the mountain geniuses: deer, birds, pumas and jaguars, serpents, rattlesnakes, all inhabitants and protectors of nature. It is theirs from the start. They will grant it style.

The Creator and Maker, displaying astonishing verbal acuity, say: "Will the animals be solitary beneath the trees? Solitude is suffering. It's convenient that, from now on, they too should be in community. Their home is the forest. Conversely, the animals make the forest whole."

Thought follows conversation. Heart of Heaven, Heart of Earth provides homes for the deer. "You, deer, shall sleep near the rivers and in the canyons of the Juyub-Taqaj, the mountain plains. You will live among the undergrowth, in the herbs. You shall walk on four feet and multiply in the forest." As this is said, shelters are provided on the land, and the deer rejoice.

Big
Nature
won. Cal-

They designate homes for birds small and large. "You shall inhabit the trees, where you will make your nests. You will shake the branches and multiply." The birds soon find their nests.

Having finished the lodging of animals, the Creator and Maker say: "Speak! Communicate with your species according to your own kind. Heart of Heaven, Heart of Earth, sanctify us by invoking our names, Juraqan, Chipi-Kakulha, and Raxa-Kakulha."

Yet it isn't possible for them to speak. They only scream, cackle, and squawk. They have no language. Each communicates according to its own fancy.

When the Creator and Maker realize their creations do not speak, they voice their displeasure: "These creatures cannot utter our name. This is not good." They add: "You shall be limited because it isn't possible for you to speak. Since you're unable to invoke us, your pasture, your habitation shall be restricted to the forests and canyons. You shall serve other creatures and be obedient. You must also accept your fate: your flesh shall be used as food."

Although the Creator and Maker rehearse again, seeking to make the animals speak, the creatures cannot understand one another. The effort is abandoned.

Another attempt by the Creator and Maker arises. "Dawn is approaching fast. How shall we succeed in being invoked, in being remembered? The creatures we made cannot praise us. Who shall utter our name? Let us now try to produce respectful beings who shall be our servants. We must sustain ourselves!"

Another creation takes place. From clay, they make human flesh. But they see that it isn't good: it is soft, motionless, shapeless, and without strength. Human heads have no depth, their faces are unbalanced. Humans cannot see, nor can they walk backward. Those creatures are able to speak but they have no understanding. It quickly becomes damp inside their heads. Humans cannot stand on their feet. And so they become undone. The Creator and Maker say: "It's clear that these creatures cannot multiply. Let us think and confer once more and decide what to do."

The Creator and Maker undo what they created. And they say: "Is there a way to complete our creation so that it acknowledges, invokes, and nourishes us? Let us tell Ixmukane and Ixpiyakok, Grandmother of Dawn and Grandfather of Day. They shall use the power of the corn kernels and *tz'ite'* seeds to decide the sustenance of humans."

Juraqan, Tepew, and Q'uq'umatz announce: "We must unite to find the means for humans to praise, sustain, and remember us. Ixmukane and Ixpiyakok, Grandmother of Dawn and Grandfather of Day, let us now make a moral human. Allow your nature to become known!

"Moral humans must distinguish between truth and lies, between right and wrong, between good and evil. Moral humans must be humble. Moral humans must change. They must grow through insight."

Ixmukane and Ixpiyakok employ their powers of divination. They ask the corn kernels and tz'ite' seeds: "Be joined in conversation by our efforts! Let it be known if it is convenient for the wooden people to be engraved. Will they invoke the Creator and Maker? Will they remember us when the day ends? If they cannot, they shall be destroyed immediately. Join forces with us. Thought must become action. Don't delay Tepew and Q'uq'umatz's efforts."

The corn kernels and tz'ite' seeds announce: "Your wooden people shall come out well. They must be given a chance to grow. They shall speak on the face of the earth. So be it."

Thus, the wooden people are ratified.

Time goes by, and with it come verb conjugations. The past becomes layered and the future unpredictable.

The wooden people looked like humans and spoke like humans. They multiplied, bearing daughters and sons. Yet they had neither soul nor understanding. And they did not remember their Creator and Maker. They were oblivious. They walked without aim on four legs.

Nor did they remember Heart of Heaven, Heart of Earth. In the end, despite the chance they were given, they were fittingly disgraced, since their creation was only a rehearsal, a failed attempt to make humans. Although they uttered words, the wooden people had no language. Nor did they have discernment. They also had no blood. Their flesh was pale.

These were the former people. Some also say they were dwarves and maybe *aluxes*, mischievous creatures still living in bushes and near temples. They lived in darkness and turned into stone. But these ideas have been discredited among the K'iche' people.

3

The wooden people were met with death. A flood caused by Heart of Heaven, Heart of Earth rotted their essence, ultimately destroying them.

The body of the first man was made of tz'ite' seeds. The body of the first woman, from *espadaña* reeds.

Yet they did not speak of their Creator and Maker either. Consequently, they too were destroyed. An abundant, boiling rain came from the sky. Xekotkowach, the turkey buzzard, flew down to empty their eyes. Camazotz, the vampire bat, arrived to decapitate them. And Kotzbalam, the jaguar, devoured them. Tukumbalam, the puma, demolished their bones and nerves. It was a just punishment because these creatures did not think of their mother and father, Heart of Heaven, Heart of Earth. The sky darkened. It rained by day and it rained by night. Boiling rain was followed by a black rain.

Small and large animals arrived in order to chastise the wooden people. Even the rocks and sticks hit them on their faces. Upset, objects rebuked them as well: water jugs, tortilla griddles, plates, grinding stones, pots and pans, even dogs. Everyone reprimanded the wooden people.

"You've caused us harm in the eyes of the Creator and Maker. Don't turn us into meat. We will eat you in return," said the animals in corrals.

The grinding stones said: "Each day and night you tormented us. Each dawn, holi, holi, huki, huki, you grind corn over our faces. You shall now suffer a similar fate. We will demolish your flesh."

The dogs spoke too: "Why wouldn't you feed us? We stared at you and you would push us away, a stick always at the ready to beat us. You treated us miserably because we could not speak. Why didn't you care? You thought only of yourselves. Why didn't you think of other beings? We shall devour you now, sinking our teeth into you."

The pots and pans, along with the tortilla griddles, grumbled: "You brought us suffering. We were constantly put to the fire. We burned mercilessly. You shall now taste that same fate."

Desperate, the wooden people ran from one place to another. They sought to climb houses but the houses collapsed and they fell to the ground along with them. They tried to climb trees but the trees resisted them. They wanted to hide in caves but the caves chose to close themselves up.

Without hope, the wooden people died. Their descendants are the monkeys in the forests. They look like humans, which is proof of their lineage.

4

Although the earth was bright, there was still neither sun nor moon. Nevertheless, Wuqub' K'aqix, known as Seven Macaws, was bragging. His presence predated the flood that destroyed the wooden people.

Wuqub' K'aqix declared himself to be the guide to those who were about to be drowned in the flood: "In dwelling above those who have been created, I am resplendent, the sun and the moon in one. My magnificence knows no end. My eyes are made of silver, glorious like jewels and emeralds. My teeth are jade stones, my beak shines from afar into the distance. When I walk away from my golden throne, the earth is illuminated."

In truth, Wuqub' K'aqix was not the sun, nor was he the moon. He only bragged about his plumage and his wealth, which was indeed made of gold and silver. His sight did not reach beyond the horizon. Nor did it extend over the entire world.

This is when the flood took place. Everything was submerged in water. Animals and all living creatures drowned. An ancient story tells of a boy who was selected to become the sun and of an old bat that opened the valleys, allowing the water to drain. But the K'iche' people know these tales are inaccurate. The next chapter details how Wuqub' K'aqix perishes.

5

The defeat of the reign of Wuqub' K'aqix's arrogance was brought about by two young men, the dazzling twins Junajpu and Ixb'alanke. The sons of Jun Junajpu and Ixkik', they are still known for their mastery of the blowgun. Their courage was without equal and so was their capacity for magic.

Junajpu, slightly older, was gorgeous. He had spots on his skin. Equally handsome, more sentimental, Ixb'alanke had darker spots on his body. They were demigods. Unparalleled masters of the blowgun, they are the founders of the K'iche' civilization. Our memory owes everything to them.

Seeing the evil caused by Wuqub' K'aqix, Junajpu and Ixb'alanke said: "Good shall never come from this, especially as humans are yet to be created. We must shoot Wuqub' K'aqix with our blowgun as he eats, causing him illness. All his wealth shall vanish: his jewels and emeralds, the gold and silver and precious metals he keeps vigil over and of which he is excessively proud. This must become a lesson. No one should be vain in the face of power."

Wuqub' K'aqix had two children: the shrewd, calculating, resourceful Sipakna, with a savvy survival instinct, and the more abrasive, temperamental Kab'raqan, who resembled an earthquake. The children were famous for their conceit. In fact, the three of them, the father and his two sons, were together known as the Prideful Gang.

Their mother was Chimalmat. Of this mythic goddess little is known.

Sipakna played in the great mountains, named Chigag, Haunahpu, Peculya, Xcanul, Macamob, and Huliznab, which are the elevations that existed at the time. Sipakna created them in one night.

Kab'raqan could move mountains. Because of him, the small and great ones would tremble. The children, along with Wuqub' K'aqix, proclaimed their greatness: "This is what I am. I am the sun," Wuqub' K'aqix announced.

"I am the one who made the earth," Sipakna stated.

"And I am he who shakes the heavens and makes tremors," Kab'raqan declared.

The twins Junajpu and Ixb'alanke did not react calmly. They perceived evil in these attitudes. They decided to plan the death of Wuqub' K'aqix, Sipakna, and Kab'raqan.

6

A ferocious battle for order and stability took place, one dependent on magic.

Wuqub' K'aqix had a *nance* tree. He ate its fruit every day, climbing the tree to fetch it. Junajpu and Ixb'alanke had spied on him. They hid at the bottom of the nance tree, in between its leaves.

When Wuqub' K'aqix arrived, he was injured by Junajpu's blowgun shot to the jaw. Screaming, he fell to the ground.

Junajpu ran quickly to capture him, but Wuqub' K'aqix outmaneuvered the brave twin. He yanked off Junajpu's arm. Pulling him to the side, he bent him from the top of the shoulder as Junajpu fought back.

Wuqub' K'aqix went home crying. He had Junajpu's arm with him. He was holding his jaw.

"What happened?" said his wife, Chimalmat.

"Those two demons shot me in the jaw with a pellet. The jaw is dislocated. My teeth are unstable. It hurts. Fortunately, I yanked off one of their arms. We can roast it over the fire. Let it hang there above the fire. Surely those demons will come to get it back."

Junajpu and Ixb'alanke thought about what to do next. They consulted with a pair of elders. The old woman was Saqi Nima Tzi and the old man, Saqi Nim Al. In truth, they were the Creator and Maker as they appear in disguise.

The twins said to them: "Come along with us to Wuqub' K'aqix's house. We shall fetch our arm from Wuqub' K'aqix. The world is yours. We will follow you. When we arrive, say we are your grandchildren. Our parents died. We always hid behind them. The only thing we know how to do is to take out the worm that causes toothaches. That's what you should tell him. This way Wuqub' K'aqix will believe we are young men eager to get advice."

"That's good," the elders said.

The four went off, the twins skipping after Saqi Nima Tzi and Saqi Nim Al. When they reached Wuqub' K'aqix's place, he was sitting on his throne, moaning in pain. He asked: "Where are you from, old folk?"

"We are hungry, Lord," Saqi Nima Tzi and Saqi Nim Al answered. "We are looking for something to eat."

"What kind of food? Are these your children who accompany you?"

"Oh no, Lord. They are our grandchildren. We feel pity for them.

We shall share whatever food you give us with them. We are looking for work. We are healers."

Wuqub' K'aqix could hardly speak because of his jaw.

"What kind of healers?"

"Lord, we pull out the worm that makes teeth hurt. We also cure the eyes and relocate the bones in their right place."

"Cure my teeth. They are making me suffer day and night. I can't find any relief. My injury was caused by two demons. They shot me with their blowgun. I can't eat. Have pity on me. Fix my teeth,"

"Very well, Lord."

Wuqub' K'aqix sat on this throne. He opened his mouth. The elders took a look. "It's a worm that is making you suffer. We must take your teeth out and replace them with new ones."

"You can't take my teeth out because I am the Lord. I have enormous wealth: jewels, gold, and silver. My ornaments are not only around me. They are in me too, in my teeth and eyes."

Saqi Nima Tzi and Saqi Nim Al replied: "We will put another set made of ground bones in its place."

Actually, the ground bones were nothing but kernels of white corn.

"Help me."

As they placed the kernels of white corn in Wuqub' K'aqix's mouth, his demeanor collapsed. He no longer looked like a lord. They also cured his eyes by blowing them off, which made his wealth disappear.

Wuqub' K'aqix no longer felt anything. Junajpu and Ixb'alanke looked on as he died, his entire wealth having vanished. He no longer had cause for his overwhelming arrogance. Chimalmat died, too.

Saqi Nima Tzi and Saqi Nim Al, undisguised now as Heart of Heaven, Heart of Earth, took back all the wealth. They dispersed it in a balanced way throughout the world.

7

One day, as Sipakna, Wuqub' K'aqix's shrewd first son and the unpredictable creator of mountains, a show-off like his father about his physical strength, was comfortably bathing in the river, he saw four hundred sweaty boys dragging a huge beam.

"What is that for?" Sipakna asked.

"It's only a beam. But it's too heavy. No matter how much we push, it's hard to move it."

"I just finished bathing. I will take it for you. What do you need it for?" Sipakna asked.

"To be the foundation of our house."

Sipakna put the beam on his shoulder and pulled it to the door where the boys planned to build their home.

They thanked him. "Stay with us now. You're smart. Where are your parents?"

"I no longer have any."

"Might we accompany you? We need to pull another log tomorrow that will also be used in the house. Might you help us?"

"Fine," Sipakna answered.

The boys came together to confer about Sipakna. "How might we defeat him?" They came up with an idea. "Let's dig a ditch right now in the structure that will become our house. Strong as he is, we will convince him that he is the most suitable candidate for going down to place the beams in the right position. Once he does, we will let one of the beams fall from above. He will die instantly. We shall have news of his death when ants surround his body as it decomposes." They proposed to celebrate at that point by drinking a sweet drink, either chicha, a beverage made of fermented berries, cane, or maize, or balche, made from fermented honey and the bark of the *balche* tree.

And so the boys dug the ditch, after which they called Sipakna.

"Please come help us dig the soil, since we cannot reach any further."

When Sipakna was at the bottom, they asked him: "Are you all the way down?"

"Yes," he answered. But, unbeknownst to the boys, he had started another hole to escape into, since he suspected they wanted to kill him. It's always advisable, when building a structure, to create alternative exits.

"Where are you?" the boys shouted.

"I'm still digging. I will let you know when I've finished the excavation."

He wasn't digging his own grave, though.

Finally, Sipakna called to the boys when he was safe in the second hole he had made.

"Come down to fetch the soil I've dug. I haven't been able to reach too far. Are you able to hear me? Your words, your screams come across as echoes, which allow me to know where you are."

The boys threw down a beam. It fell to the bottom of the hole, causing thunder.

"Let no one speak," they said as they waited. No sound came. "The demon is dead. We've been successful. The ants will confirm what our hearts already know." Overjoyed, the boys threw a party: "Let's drink our sweet drink for the next three days."

As they became drunk, ants quietly started to invade the construction. The boys didn't see them.

Sipakna listened to their feast from afar. He also saw the ants. On the second day, the ants arrived in greater numbers, coming and going everywhere, through the holes and around the beams. The boys realized the ants were carrying a few fragments of Sipakna's nails and hair.

"This proves our belief: he is gone!" they said.

Sipakna had realized the boys were drinking. He thought he would let them lose their strength and become drunk. Meanwhile, he would cut some of his hair and nails for the ants to take as evidence of his demise.

When the boys were nearly unconscious, Sipakna climbed up from the ditch and toppled the structure on top of them. All of them were crushed when the roof collapsed. No one survived except Sipakna, who was proud of his display of shrewdness.

The boys became the four hundred stars known in the Mayan language as Motz, which is the Pleiades constellation.

8

No amount of ingenuity from Sipakna, son of Wuqub' K'aqix, however, was a match for the astounding creativity of Junajpu and Ixb'alanke, who were upset after he killed the four hundred boys.

Sipakna ate fish and crab daily. The twins decided to create a figure that looked like a crab. They used bromeliad flower to make the claws. For the shell, they hollowed out a stone. They put the shell at the bottom of a cave below the great mountain called Meauan.

Their blowguns at the ready, the twins went to look for Sipakna at the edge of the river.

"Where are you going?" they asked him.

"Nowhere," he answered. "I'm looking for my food."

"What type of food?"

"Fish and crab. But there is none here, or I haven't found any. I haven't eaten since the day before yesterday, and I'm starving."

"At the bottom of the canyon there is a crab," the twins said, "a very big one. It's your food. It beat us when we tried to catch it, so we are afraid. Otherwise, we would go get it."

"I beg you to have pity on me. Show it to me," Sipakna said.

"We don't want to. Go alone! You will not get lost. Follow the path of the river and you shall reach a great mountain. The crab is making noise at the bottom of the canyon. You only have to get there," Junajpu and Ixb'alanke said.

"Ah, what misfortune. You can't find it in yourselves to accompany me? Come along. There are many birds you can catch with the blowgun."

His humility convinced the twins. He even cried before them. They said: "Perhaps you will not be able to catch it. Then you'll have to return, as we did after it bit us. We went headfirst but couldn't catch it. We crawled on our stomachs. We suggest that you go lying on your back."

"Very well," Sipakna said, who sometimes looked like a crocodile. He went with them.

The three arrived at the bottom of the canyon. The crab was on one side with its red shell.

"That's good," Sipakna said, salivating. "I can't wait to eat it." He disappeared into the cave, where he tried crawling headfirst. But the crab climbed back up and Sipakna retreated, coming out of the cave empty-handed.

"Did you catch it?"

"No," he answered. It climbed and I couldn't grab it. It might be better if I reach it faceup."

Sipakna entered the cave again. This time only his feet were visible to the twins.

At this point the great mountain of Meauan collapsed on Sipakna's chest. It was a colossal death. Sipakna was swallowed up by the mountain, becoming stone inside it.

9

The third member of the Prideful Gang was Wuqub' K'aqix's second son, Kab'raqan, whose every move was like a tremor.

"It is my will that Kab'raqan be humbled as well," Heart of Heaven, Heart of Earth told Junajpu and Ixb'alanke.

"Very well," the twins answered.

Kab'raqan entertained himself by shaking mountains. Even the smallest of his steps fractured them. That is how Junajpu and Ixb'alanke found him.

They asked Kab'raqan: "Where are you going?"

"Nowhere," he answered. "I'm moving mountains, bringing them down forever."

Kab'raqan asked the twins: "Why are you here? I've never seen your faces. What are your names?"

"We have no names," they responded. "We do nothing but shoot our blowguns. We are poor and own nothing. We simply like walking up and down the mountains. And we've seen a huge mountain. It's the highest mountain we know. We haven't been able to climb it, which means we haven't hunted even one bird on it. Is it true you can knock down every mountain?"

"Have you really seen such a mountain?" Kab'raqan wondered. "Where is it? Once I see it, I will bring it down. Where did you see it?"

"Where the sun is born."

"Point the way for me."

"It will be better if we accompany you," Junajpu and Ixb'alanke said, "one of us on your left side, the other on the right. We have blowguns, which we want to use to hunt birds."

Kab'raqan agreed and the three proceeded. The twins used their blowguns every time they saw a bird. They used no pellets; their sheer breath brought down the prey. Kab'raqan was amazed at their skill.

They stopped, built a fire, and grilled the prey they'd caught. They covered the birds with *tizate*, a poisonous white chalklike powder, until they were coated with white earth.

"The smell will stir Kab'raqan's appetite," they said. "The moment he eats the poison, he himself will be ready to be buried in the earth. Great is the wisdom of Heart of Heaven, Heart of Earth."

"What you're cooking smells delicious," Kab'raqan affirmed. "Please share it with me."

The twins gave him a portion. He devoured it. As soon as they continued their trek, Kab'raqan felt sick. His hands and feet began to shake and he quickly lost all his strength.

Junajpu and Ixb'alanke proceeded to tie his hands behind his back and his neck and feet together, and threw him to the ground. He died shortly after. The twins buried him on the spot.

The reign of Wuqub' K'aqix, Sipakna, and Kab'raqan was thus brought to an end.

Part II: Xibalba

1

These ancient stories move now to the underworld.

Junajpu and Ixb'alanke's father, Jun Junajpu, was also a twin. His brother was Wuqub' Junajpu. They were wise and could foresee the future. Their own parents were Ixpiyakok and Ixmukane.

Jun Junajpu had two older sons, Jun B'atz' and Jun Ch'owem, who played the flute, sang, painted, sculpted, made jewelry and silver artifacts, and were also dexterous with the blowgun. Their mother was Ixbaquiyalo, bearer of monkeys.

Jun Junajpu and Wuqub' Junajpu were wise. They enjoyed playing dice and ball every day. The four of them, father, uncle, and older sons, would pair off to oppose each other.

A falcon who was among the numerous messengers from Xibalba, the underworld, once watched them play. He reported to Juraqan. The falcon could fly to the underworld and back with no trouble.

Xibalba is the site of fear, a magisterial city, with palaces and a torture-dome, gardens, and an oracular window where time comes to a standstill. Those unfortunate eyes who have been fated to see it describe the oracular window as irradiating unbearable darkness.

The underworld is made of countless roads leading everywhere and nowhere. The entrance is a cave in Coban, Guatemala, although there are other cave systems in nearby Belize and Chiapas. The map of Xibalba is ciphered in the Milky Way.

Nobody enters Xibalba, for there are innumerable obstacles and traps, including a river of scorpions. There is also a crossroads where visitors must choose among four paths, all of which lead to a parallel world where up is down, light is darkness, cold is warm, and good is evil. There are effigies near them, awaiting those who have not yet lost their minds. A special chamber is reserved for the white, bearded men.

Among the wonders of Xibalba is its eternal mutability. Every time a traveler describes it, the place changes. To some, it is reminiscent of their own cities of origin; to others, it's like no place in the natural world.

Upon hearing about it, several white, bearded men who preached Christendom tried to enter it without success. The only one to emerge lost his mind. In his last written testimony, he said the darkness of Xibalba is of such depth, it's like entreating the heart of Heart of Heaven, Heart of Earth.

In Xibalba, death is life.

The falcon serving as messenger described what he saw to the supreme lawmakers of Xibalba, Jun Kame, and Ququb' Kame. After gathering in council, these lords said: "Who is it who allows the earth to tremble, making such a racket? Go call them! Let them come here to play ball, where we can defeat them. They don't respect us. They have no consideration for our kind."

There were other lords in Xibalba, twelve in total: Xixiripat and Kuchumakik, who caused people to vomit. Ajalpuj and Ajalkana' made pus ooze from the skin of the legs and face, which would become yellow with jaundice. Chamiyab'aq and Chamiyajom, the sheriffs of Xibalba, made people lose weight, turning them into calaveras. Ajalmes and Ajaltoqt'ob caused heart attacks. The role of Kik'xik and Patan was to provoke accidents on the road. They would simply wear out people's necks and hearts. All this is known to K'iche' people, who believe illnesses are brought about by the underworld lords.

As they all gathered, they looked for a way to torment Jun Junajpu and Wuqub' Junajpu. What the lords of Xibalba wanted was their gear for playing ball: their leather; their yokes, from which the ball bounced in the process of playing the game; their gloves; as well as their adorned face masks. The ball game was a noisy affair.

The lords of Xibalba were envious.

2

The lords of Xibalba sent four owl messengers. The owls had distinct characteristics: one was able to pierce like an agile arrow, the second one had only one leg, the third had a red back, and the fourth had a skull with no legs. The four left Xibalba and aligned themselves atop the ballcourt, which was bounded by high stone walls. They delivered the message from the lords of Xibalba to Jun Junajpu and Wuqub' Junajpu.

"Have the lords truly spoken that way?"

"Yes," the owls replied. "We must accompany you. Bring your gear. You'll be asked to play ball."

Jun Junajpu and Wuqub' Junajpu pondered. They decided to go, leaving behind Jun Junajpu's sons, Jun B'atz' and Jun Ch'owem, whose mother, Ixbaquiyalo, had died by then.

"We must say farewell to our mother. We shall also leave our rubber ball behind." They hung it from the ceiling. They said: "We will come back and play."

On their way out, Jun B'atz' and Jun Ch'owem were instructed: "Heat your home and warm your grandmother's heart."

When they said goodbye to their mother, Jun Ch'owem started to cry. "Don't worry," his father and uncle said. "We must go, but do not grieve for us, because we won't die."

Jun Junajpu and Wuqub' Junajpu left together with the owls. On their way to Xibalba, they descended a steep ladder that led to a labyrinth. They reached the edge of an underground river that made its way through the canyons called Nuzivan Kul and Cuzivan, which they crossed. They walked along several more rivers, one of them filled with scorpions. The scorpions were many, but the men eluded being injured.

They soon arrived at the river of blood, and this one they also crossed without drinking from its waters. Then they overcame the river of pus. They conquered them all, but not without a creeping anxiety. Were they trapped?

They came to a four-path crossroads. Of the paths, one was red, another black, a third was white, and a fourth yellow. Each path was an entrance to a different dimension: in one, tall is short; in the second, day is night; in the third, summer is winter; and in the fourth, criminals are honorable. It is the belief of the K'iche' people that the crossroads are extremely dangerous. Unseen powers become seen. Likewise, the cardinal directions are associated with colors: white with north, red with east, yellow with south, and black with west. Candles must be lit in these four points to delimit the corners of nature.

The black path spoke: "Take me, for I am the lord's road."

This is where the first set of heroic twins was defeated. They were taken through the path of Xibalba and arrived at the council of lords, where they were greeted.

The first entities they saw were dummies, made of sticks. They had been arranged by the lords of Xibalba.

Those who were seated first were effigies.

"How are you?" an effigy said.

Frightened, Jun Junajpu and Wuqub' Junajpu did not respond.

They slowly began to converse with the effigies.

"Greetings, Jun Kame and Ququb' Kame."

At this point, seeing the twins talking to effigies, the lords of Xibalba burst out laughing.

"Sit down," they ordered.

Naive, the twins sat down on a scorching bench and got burned.

The lords laughed again. Jun Kame and Ququb' Kame spoke: "We're glad you've come. Prepare your gear for tomorrow. You'll be taken to the House of Darkness, where you will be given a torch made of resinous *ocote* pine as well as a cigar. Light the torch as well as your cigar, but remember that tomorrow you must return these items to us."

The twins agreed. They arrived at the House of Darkness. There was nothing but darkness in it.

Meanwhile, the lords of Xibalba discussed what to do next. "The way they play instruments will be useful for us. The moment they make a mistake they will be doomed. We will sacrifice them tomorrow."

Jun Junajpu and Wuqub' Junajpu were meditating when a messenger brought them the torch and cigar. Since the torch was already burning, they used it to light the cigar. "Don't let these items burn. You can't use them up. They must be returned in the morning."

This is a description of the trials of Xibalba, which are numerous and acquire many shapes.

The first is the House of Darkness, *Quequema-ha*.

The second is the House of Tremors, *Xuxulim-ha*. It's extremely cold inside.

The third is the House of Jaguars, *Balami-ha*. There are only jaguars roaming in it, snarling and stepping on each other.

Zotzi-ha, the House of Bats, is the fourth punishing place. It's full of bats that flutter. None is able to leave.

The fifth place is the House of Blades, *Chayn-ha*, full of sharp, cutting blades made either of flint or obsidian stone, which is a dark volcanic glass with a razor-sharp edge.

There are many other sites of torment in Xibalba. I prefer to mention only these few.

Next morning, when Jun Junajpu and Wuqub' Junajpu returned before Jun Kame and Ququb' Kame, they were asked: "Where are the cigars? And the ocote torch?"

"We consumed them."

"You've failed the test. Today shall be your last day. We'll cut you to pieces and your memory will be erased."

Sadly, that's indeed what happened. The first set of twins was sacrificed and buried in Pukbal, a word that refers to the dust that becomes visible during an intense game. The head of Jun Junajpu was cut off. The rest of his body was buried with his younger brother Wuqub' Junajpu.

"Take the head and place it in a tall tree planted on the road," Jun Kame and Ququb' Kame ordered.

That tree had never borne fruit until Jun Junajpu's head was hung in it. It is the tree known today as calabash, a type of squash. It's apparent to anyone who enters Xibalba. The head never appeared again after it became the fruit.

This is why in K'iche' cemeteries the rows of graves bear trees, making them look like groves.

The lords of Xibalba ordered: "Let no one cut the fruit. Nor should anyone be under the tree from now on. It shall be a monument to our victory."

3

This is the story of Princess Ixkik', who, upon hearing the story of the calabash tree, reached it and wanted to touch it.

She was the daughter of Kuchumakik.

"Will I die if I touch the fruits? Surely they must be delicious."

She was soon on her way to Pukbal, alone. "Isn't it beautiful how the tree is covered with fruit?"

A calavera hiding behind the tree popped up: "These fruits are actually calaveras. Do you want them?"

"Yes, I do," she replied.

"Let me have your right hand," the calavera said.

Ixkik' extended her right hand. At that moment, the calavera spit on it. As she looked at it, the spit vanished.

"It is my saliva. My spit has given you my offspring. Go back up to Earth. You shall not die, trust me," the calavera said. "The head is beautiful while alive.

But after death people become frightened of it. Beauty vanishes and only bones remain. In a similar way, a child is like saliva: the parent's essence is in it. The face of his parents is in the child's, although at times one must look hard to find it. Death is final but survival takes place through progeny. That progeny is already in our body, in ourselves."

The princess returned home pregnant. That is how Junajpu and Ixb'alanke were conceived.

After six months, her condition was seen by her father, called Kuchumakik.

The lords of Xibalba, Jun Kame and Ququb' Kame, along with Kuchumakik, gathered together to reflect on the situation.

"My daughter is with child," her father said. "She has been dishonored."

"Force her to speak the truth. If she refuses to speak, sacrifice her by tearing her heart from her chest."

Kuchumakik questioned his daughter: "Whose child are you carrying?" She answered: "I'm not carrying a child. I have known no man."

"Take her to be sacrificed," he told the four owls, who are the most important messengers of Xibalba. "Bring me back her heart in this bowl."

The four messengers took the bowl. They flew away carrying Princess Ixkik' in their wings. They also took with them the stone knife for the sacrifice.

Ixkik' told the owls: "Don't kill me. It is no dishonor what I carry in my womb. It was conceived as I admired the tree where the head of Jun Junajpu was placed in Pukbal."

"And what shall we substitute your heart with?" the owls wondered. We don't want to die."

"Do not worry. You no longer will lure people to death, nor will your home be in Xibalba. The cycle of life is inescapable. Death is connected with birth, and vice versa. For maize to grow, a seed must die and be buried in the soil. Take the sap from this *chik'te'* tree," said the young woman.

The red sap emerging from that tree fell into the bowl, oozing into a substitute for the heart of Ixkik'. It soon became resplendent. The K'iche' use the hearts of large animals—jaguars, pumas, crocodiles—for offerings, throwing them into the fire to burn. If those animals are not available, they make hearts out of incense. The chik'te' tree was called the Sacrificial Red Tree. She named the coagulation blood. The tree is still called blood croton.

The princess said to the owls: "On Earth, you'll be precious."

"We shall rise to serve you," the messengers replied. "Follow your own road while we bring the sap before the lords."

When the owls arrived, everyone was waiting for them, Kuchumakik' most attentively.

"Have your duties been fulfilled?" Jun Kame asked.

"Everything was done according to your commands. The heart is in the bowl."

"Let us see," Jun Kame exclaimed. The heart appeared red and full of blood, although it was only sap.

"Make a fire and place it over the embers," Jun Kame ordered.

The owls immediately tossed the heart into the fire, as is custom among the K'iche'. The odor that emerged was the smell of Xibalba.

As the lords cherished the sight, the owls opened their wings and rose from the abyss toward the earth, where they are beloved.

4

Jun B'atz' and Jun Ch'owem were visiting with their grandmother when Princess Ixkik' arrived. She had the twins in her womb. It wasn't long before Junajpu and Ixb'alanke were born.

When Ixkik' came before the grandmother, she announced: "I'm your daughter-in-law."

She did what new K'iche' brides still do, which is moving into the home of their mother-in-law to ensure they learn the necessary skills to carry on the family tradition. But Ixkik' was no conventional bride. She was a poet. Every word that came from her mouth was infused with beauty.

At night, she had pleasing dreams. When she woke, she would sing to them. These are some of her verses:

We rise from sleep
and in dreams we give birth.
We dream of home
and in life we build that house.

"Where are you coming from?" asked the grandmother "Where are my children? Are they dead in Xibalba? You will never be my daughter-in-law."

"It's true that I am your daughter-in-law. I'm carrying twins. They are the sons of Jun Junajpu. I carry them inside me. Jun Junajpu and Wuqub' Junajpu are not dead. They shall reveal themselves again. You'll soon see your oldest son's image in what I carry inside me."

Jun B'atz' and Jun Ch'owem were musicians. They entertained themselves with playing the flute and singing, painting, and sculpting. All day long. They comforted their grandmother.

The grandmother said: "You're an impostor."

"They are truly his. I am part of your family," Ixkik' replied.

Finally, the grandmother said: "If you are indeed my daughter-in-law, go fetch food for those who need to be fed. Plant a net full of maize and come right back, since you're my daughter-in-law."

It is common in K'iche' society for a new bride to be handed heavy tasks by her in-laws to prove her abilities.

"Very well."

Ixkik' slept deeply that night. In a dream, she saw the inside of her womb.

In the morning, she immediately left for the maize field that belonged to Jun B'atz' and Jun Ch'owem. The road had been cleared for her. There was only a single ear of maize in the field, though. She became anxious.

"Ah, I'm a sinner. I feel disgraced. Where shall I go to find the net full of maize that was asked of me?"

She invoked Kah'al and the guardians of food to arrive: Ixta', Ixkanil, and Iskak'au.

"You who cook the maize. And you, Kah'al, guardian of the food for Jun B'atz' and Jun Ch'owem." She took hold of the corn silk, pulling it upward. As she placed them in the maize net, it suddenly became full with ears of corn.

As Ixkik' came back, she sang a poem:

Children of maize
our past is your future.
Children of maize
your strength is our faith.

The animals of the field carried the maize net. They placed it in a corner of the house as if the daughter-in-law had carried the net herself.

When the grandmother realized the quantity of ears of corn before her, she said:

Where have you found that maize? Did you destroy our family maize field? I will go check right away."

The only plant of maize was still in its place.

The grandmother came back: "You sing poems of truth. You have shown you are truly my daughter-in-law. I shall now watch over you, and those you carry in your womb, who are also wise."

5

Soon after Ixkik' gave birth to Junajpu and Ixb'alanke—the former was holding the latter's ankle when they came out of the womb—their grandmother grew angry hearing them cry night and day.

"They are never at peace," she said. "Throw them out."

Jun B'atz' and Jun Ch'owem were jealous, not accepting them in the house. The second set of twins was therefore placed on top of an anthill on the mountain, where they slept comfortably. From there they were then placed atop thorns, but they continued to enjoy themselves.

Their older brothers had become great flutists and singers. They had overcome misfortune and were now sages. They were also excellent writers and carvers. They did everything successfully. But their envy took away the best of them.

The grandmother didn't love them either. Only when Jun B'atz' and Jun Ch'owem had finished eating were the twins fed. They did not get enraged or angry, though. They suffered stoically because they understood their own condition, and this was the light by which they could see.

Junajpu and Ixb'alanke' spent the whole day with their blowguns. They nurtured the thought of running away.

One day, the twins came back without a single catch. As they entered the house, their grandmother berated them.

"The birds become stuck in trees. We cannot climb to fetch them. If our older brothers want, let them come with us to bring down the birds."

"We shall go with you at sunrise," the older siblings answered.

The twins consulted on how to give Jun B'atz' and Jun Ch'owem a lesson. "We shall merely overturn their nature. This is the essence of our words. For if it had been according to their desires, we, their younger siblings, would have died."

They arrived at the bottom of the tree called *can'te*, a type of cacao from which a yellow dye is extracted. Their blowguns in hand, Junajpu and Ixb'alanke' were accompanied by their older siblings.

It wasn't possible to count the number of birds on that tree. The older siblings were in awe. Yet none would fall.

"Go up to fetch them," the twins told Jun B'atz' and Jun Ch'owem.

"Fine," they answered as the older siblings climbed the tree. Its trunk suddenly grew to three times its previous size.

Seeing this, Jun B'atz' wanted to climb down but could not. They said from atop: What happened to us is a misfortune. We are even afraid of looking at the can'te."

Junajpu and Ixb'alanke replied: "Untie your loincloths, then retie them under your waists. Let the ends loose and pull from them from behind. It will allow you to move easily."

The older siblings let their loincloths loose. But soon they became tails, giving them the appearance of monkeys. They automatically started to jump from one branch to another, traversing mountains great and small. They went into the forest, making apelike gestures. This is the origin of the dance Palo Volador, in which dancers climb a pole and, with their ankles tied to a rope, spin downward.

Miraculously, Junajpu and Ixb'alanke had defeated them. When the twins came back home, they spoke with their grandmother as well as with their mother: "The faces of our siblings became those of animals."

"If you've done them harm, I will be disgraced," the grandmother said.

The twins replied: "You shall see them again. But it'll be a difficult test: be careful not to laugh."

They went into the jungle and played on the flute the song "Junajpu Spider Monkey." Jun B'atz' and Jun Ch'owem heard them and were lured back home. When the grandmother saw their monkey faces, their big bottoms, their thin tails and the hole in their waist, she wasn't able to contain her laughter.

The twins left for the jungle again. "What shall we do now?"

They again played the flute and the monkeys returned. In total, they tried to bring Jun B'atz' and Jun Ch'owem four times. It happened the same way.

The twins told their grandmother: "We've done everything possible. But don't worry. We are your grandchildren, too. You should see us: we are the memory of our older siblings. Do not worry: we assure you that musicians and singers will invoke them, the houses they built, the music they played, and how they became monkeys."

6

The efforts by the twins to be better known by their grandmother and mother began almost right away. The first thing they did was work in the cornfield, or at least they pretended to. Their magical powers took care of most of it.

As soon as Junajpu and Ixb'alanke applied picks to the soil, the picks would start digging on their own. The same with their axes, which would chop down trees without them making any effort. It was impossible to count the number of trees that were cut that way.

Excited, the twins asked the dove Ixmukur to keep an eye out. Their command was clear: as soon as their grandmother showed up, she should coo.

With their blowguns, Junajpu and Ixb'alanke left in order to hunt. Soon Ixmukur started to coo, and they ran back. One of the twins immediately covered his hands and face in mud to appear like a laborer. The other one threw slivers of wood on his head so it looked like he had been cutting trees.

Their grandmother saw through the pretense, though. Although at noon they ate what she had cooked for them, she knew they really hadn't done much of the labor themselves. In her eyes, they did not deserve the food.

Junajpu and Ixb'alanke were undeterred. When they came home that night, they said as they stretched their legs and arms, "We are truly tired."

To the twins' surprise, the next day, when they returned to the cornfield, they discovered that all the trees that had been cut the day before were all standing once again in their original places.

"Who is playing tricks on us?" they asked. Animals small and large had done this to them: the puma, the jaguar, the deer, the rabbit, the bobcat, the coyote, the wild hog, the peccary, or the coati. In a single night, they together brought the cornfield to its original state.

When they returned home, they told their grandmother: "What do you think? The cornfield we had labored has once again been covered with grass and a thick forest. It isn't fair."

At sunset, after pondering, they went back. Then they decided to hide in order to catch their adversaries. "We may be able to surprise those who come to do harm," they said. They camouflaged themselves, hiding in a special place under the shade.

It was midnight when Junajpu and Ixb'alanke saw all the animals coming together, one of each species, saying in unison: "Arise, trees. Come back, bushes."

The twins were amazed. They tried catching the puma and the jaguar but these just ran off. They came close to the deer and the rabbit, able to grab their tails before they fled. For that reason, to this day the rabbit and deer have short tails.

The bobcat, the coyote, the wild hog, the peccary, and the coati did not give up either. These animals paraded in front of Junajpu and Ixb'alanke, whose hearts were troubled because they couldn't catch them.

Finally, the rat came down, scurrying. They caught it and wrapped it in a net. They squeezed the rat behind the head, trying to strangle it. They burned its tail over a fire. This is why the rat doesn't have a hairy tail.

The rat said: "I shall not die in your hands. Your trade isn't that of maize farmers."

"What are you saying?" the twins wanted to know.

"First let me go," the rat said. "I have something I want to say to you. I will say it after you give me something to eat."

"Speak first. You'll get your food later," they said.

"It's about the goods that your father and uncle, Jun Junajpu and Wuqub' Junajpu, who died in Xibalba, left hanging from beneath the roof of the house," the rat said. "Their yokes, their gloves, and their rubber ball. Your grandmother doesn't want to show these items to you because your father and uncle died as a result of them."

"Is it true?" the twins asked. Their hearts rejoiced when they heard about the rubber ball. Since the rat had already spoken, they presented it with some food: grains of maize, squash seeds, chili pepper, beans, *pataxte*, and cacao. "All this belongs to you. If there is something that is stored or forgotten, it will be yours forever. Eat it!"

"Wonderful," the rat said. "What shall I tell your grandmother if she sees me?"

"Don't worry, because we are here. We know what to say to her. Let's get to that corner of the house to fetch the items our father and uncle left for us."

The twins spent the night reflecting and discussing. It was noon when they returned home with the rat. One of the twins entered the house discreetly and the other hid outside. They made the rat climb up.

Junajpu and Ixb'alanke then asked their grandmother for food: "We want chili sauce." She cooked their food. They each got a bowl.

This was done to fool their grandmother and mother. They drained the water jug into a pot so that their grandmother had to go down to the river to fetch more water. On the surface of the chili sauce and on the pan containing the drained water, the twins saw the reflection of the rat going in the direction of the rubber ball hanging from the roof.

They asked a mosquito called Xan, which is similar to a small biting fly, to go to the river and perforate the jug their grandmother was carrying. When she raised the jug, water leaked from it. She couldn't see the perforation.

"What's happening to our grandmother? Our mouths are dry from so much thirst," the twins said to their mother. They sent her down to the river as well.

The rat soon cut the string from which the rubber ball was hanging. Down came the yokes, the gloves, the leather, and the rubber ball. Junajpu and Ixb'alanke took them and ran to hide them on the road that led to the ball field.

After this, the twins went to the river to reunite with their grandmother and mother, who were busy trying to stop the water in the jug from spilling. They each had their blowgun. "What are you doing? We got tired of waiting."

"Look at the hole in the jug. We can't cover it," the women said.

The twins repaired it and together they returned home, first Ixb'alanke, then Junajpu, with their grandmother and mother behind them. This is how the twins found the rubber ball. The K'iche' people venerate an elderly female god named Ixchel who is depicted with a jug from which she pours out water in the form of rain. She is the patroness of childbirth.

7

The hero twins happily went to the court to play ball. They played for a long time. It was the same court where their father and uncle used to play.

The lords of Xibalba heard about them: "Who are those who once again play over our heads and bother us with the racket they make, just like Jun Junajpu and Wuqub' Junajpu, who were eager to vanquish us?"

They told their ferocious hyenas, who served as messengers, "Go tell them to come, by order of the lords. We want to play ball with them in seven days."

The hyenas took a winding road up and out of Xibalba and into the world. They followed rivers across mountains until they reached the twins' house, where they found the grandmother.

She was taken aback. "Junajpu and Ixb'alanke are wanted by the lords," the hyenas announced imperiously. "In seven days' time."

The grandmother felt a tremor inside her. She was anxious and without words. Her legs were about to collapse. Yet she quickly replied, "They shall be there."

When the hyenas left, she didn't know what to do. "Who shall I ask to call the twins? Wasn't this exactly the way the owls of Xibalba came the last time and took away their father and uncle?"

She was alone and afflicted at home. While she was wandering around, a louse fell out of her head and into her lap. She lifted it and put the louse on her palm. It moved around and began to talk.

"What is it that concerns you?" the louse said.

"Go fetch my grandchildren from the court. Tell them that messengers of Xibalba have come before their grandmother. They are required to show up in seven days."

On the road to the court, the louse came across a toad called Tamazul.

"Where are you going?" the toad said.

"I have a command to fulfill. I need to fetch Junajpu and Ixb'alanke," the louse answered.

"I don't see why you need to hurry," Tamazul stated. "Do you want me to swallow you? You'll see how I jump. We shall get there together to the court faster than you might on your own."

"Fine," the louse answered. The toad swallowed the louse, then leaped as far as possible without hurrying. He came across a snake called Sakikas.

"Where are you going, Tamazul?" Sakikas asked the toad.

"I'm an envoy. I have a message to deliver inside my belly."

"I see you are in no hurry. Wouldn't I arrive faster?" the snake said. "I can swallow you and arrive quickly."

Sakikas devoured Tamazul.

The snake was going quickly when she was met by a sparrow hawk named Lotz'kik, which is closely related to the falcon *Oactli*. The sparrow hawk ate the snake.

The sparrow hawk landed on a cornice near the court where Junajpu and Ixb'alanke were playing. "Vak-ko, vak-ko," it said, which means "Here is the hawk!"

"Why are you making such noise?" the twins said. "Let us get our blowguns."

They immediately shot the sparrow hawk, hitting it in the eye. It fell and they ran to get it. "What are you doing here?" they wanted to know.

"I have a message in my belly."

"Speak up."

"Cure my eye first and I will give it to you," the sparrow hawk said.

Junajpu and Ixb'alanke took a bit of the rubber ball and placed it on the bird's eye. The sparrow hawk's injury was cured instantly.

"Again, speak up," they repeated.

The sparrow hawk spat out the snake.

"Speak up," the twins told the snake.

"Fine," she said as she vomited the toad.

"Where is the message you are carrying?" they asked the toad.

"It's in my belly," the toad answered as it tried but failed to let the louse out. Its mouth became filled with saliva. The young men wanted to punish the toad.

"You're a liar," they said. The toad again tried to spit out the louse but only saliva filled its mouth.

Junajpu and Ixb'alanke opened the toad's mouth themselves and looked inside. The louse was stuck on the toad's teeth. He had stayed there all the time but pretended to have been swallowed. In other words, the toad was fooled. This is why toads don't taste what they eat. They are the food of snakes.

The louse symbolizes decay. The toad is associated with the fertility of the earth. The serpent signifies regeneration. And the falcon announces the reborn sun at dawn.

"Speak up," Junajpu and Ixb'alanke told the louse.

The louse responded: "Your grandmother asked me to get you. Hyenas serving as messengers for Jun Kame and Ququb' Kame have asked you to go to Xibalba. They said, 'In seven days, they must come to play ball with us. Let them bring their playing tools: the rubber ball, the yokes, the gloves, and the leather to be competitive.' Your grandmother spoke with cries and laments."

Seven are the levels of the earth that exist above the underworld.

"Is it possible?" the twins said to themselves when they heard the news.

A LARIOS

As they returned home, they thought about the command. Frightened as they were, they made up their minds to go to Xibalba. They were just going home to say goodbye.

"We are departing," Junajpu and Ixb'alanke said to their grandmother and mother. "A sign of our fate shall remain with you, though. Each of us shall plant a stalk of *caña*, unripe maize, right in the middle of our house. If it dries up, it will mean that we are dead. But if the caña sprouts, you'll know that we are alive. And you, mother, don't cry. We go where our father and uncle went before us."

First Ixb'alanke planted his caña, then Junajpu planted his. They planted them inside the house and not in the field, not in humid soil but on dry land.

8

The twins marched forward, each with their blowgun. They crossed mountains until they descended a staircase in the direction of Xibalba. As they went down, they passed by canyons and rivers. They also came across birds called Molay.

They should have died in those rivers but survived by navigating them on top of their blowguns. They arrived at a four-path crossroads they knew about: black, white, red, and yellow.

The boys sent the mosquito called Xan to fly ahead of them. "Suck the blood of those you meet," the boys commanded.

Through back roads, Xan came across wooden puppets that were like the wooden people first created by Heart of Heaven, Heart of Earth: pale, innocuous, without soul. Yet unlike them, these puppets were covered with ornaments. He stung the first, but it did not speak a word. The mosquito stung another sitting nearby. This one didn't speak either.

"Ay," Jun Kame exclaimed in pain, after being stung.

"What is it, Jun Kame? What stung you?" the lord next to him asked. Realizing the lords were evil, the mosquito went on a rampage.

"Ay," Ququb' Kame screamed.

"What happened, Ququb' Kame? What stung you?" the fifth lord sitting in that row said.

"Ay," Kuchumakik' said.

"What happened, Kuchumakik'? What stung you?" the sixth lord said.

"Ay," Xixiripat said.

"What happened, Xixiripat? What stung you?" the seventh lord said.

It went on this way for some time.

"What happened, Ajalpuj?"

"What happened, Chamiyab'aq?"

"What happened, Ajalkana'?"

"What happened, Chamiyajom?"

"What happened, Patan?"

"What happened, Kik'xik'?"

"What happened, Ajalmes?"

"What happened, Ajaltoqt'ob?"

Thus they enunciated their names. They revealed themselves that way, calling each other lord. Not one of their names was omitted.

The twins continued along their road until they came to where the lords sat among the effigies, as they had learned from Xan.

"Greet the lords," a voice said.

"These are no lords, but wooden puppets," the twins replied.

The twins started to sweat. Then they called out to hail them:

"Greetings to Jun Kame! Greetings to Ququb' Kame! Greetings to Xixiripat! . . ." The twins went around greeting each of the lords by name.

"Sit down," the twins were told as the lords pointed in the direction of a burning stone.

"That isn't a seat," the twins replied.

They weren't about to be fooled like their father and uncle had been.

"Go to that house," the lords requested. The twins looked at the place: it was the House of Darkness.

9

This was their first test in Xibalba.

When the twins entered the House of Darkness, the lords of Xibalba thought they were about to defeat Junajpu and Ixb'alanke.

They were given an ocote torch and a cigar. "Light them up but don't let them burn," the lords ordered. "Return them to us unconsumed tomorrow morning at sunrise."

The twins did not light the ocote torch and cigar. Instead, they put red macaw tail feathers on the tip of the torch, making it look as if its tip was in flames. And they placed a cluster of fireflies at the end of the cigar to bring about the same effect.

Meanwhile, the lords were confident this second set of twins would perform exactly as the first had. But in the morning, the messengers reported that neither object had been consumed. They reported the news to the lords.

"How is it possible? Where have they come from? Who created them? Who brought them to the world? They make our hearts burn with ire. It is not good what they do to us. Their faces are strange. Strange also is the way they conduct themselves."

The twins kept their secret.

The lords asked Junajpu and Ixb'alanke to come before them: "Let's play ball," Jun Kame and Ququb' Kame said.

"We agree," the twins replied.

The lords tossed the ball.

"Where do you come from?"

"We don't know where we come from!"

"We shall use our rubber ball," the lords of Xibalba said.

"No," the twins responded. "We will use ours."

"We refuse," the lords declared.

"Fine."

The lords of Xibalba threw the ball directly into Junajpu's ring. And as soon as they took hold of the knives of stone to tear the twins to pieces, the ball started to bounce along the entire ballcourt.

"You aren't playing fairly!" the twins said, as they continued shouting and stomping, which annoyed the lords of Xibalba. "You want to kill us? Did you not ask us to come? Didn't your own messengers come to find us? May you be disgraced. We shall leave immediately."

"Don't leave, young men. Let's continue playing ball. Now we can use yours."

As soon as Junajpu and Ixb'alanke got out their own rubber ball, their dexterity in the court had a fulminating effect. The game was quickly over.

Hurt by the defeat, the lords of Xibalba said: "Don't think this is the end. We order you to fetch a bouquet of red *chipilín*, one of white chipilín, one of yellow chipilín, and one of large petals. Tomorrow morning, we shall play ball again."

The chipilín is a plant with edible leaves that makes those who ingest it sleepy.

Their conversation concluded. Junajpu and Ixb'alanke had been strong and energetic in their words. Their hearts were serene. Yet the lords of Xibalba were convinced their luck had run out.

As they went about to find the flowers, they entered the House of Blades, the second place of torment in Xibalba. The blades talked to them: "You'll only be allowed to cut animal flesh."

The hero twins were careful not to move inside that chamber. In an attempt to escape, they summoned a battalion of ants—black ants and army ants: cutting ants. "Bring us marigolds, plumeria, and other *kotzij* [the word for flower and also placenta] grown by the lords."

The ants left in search of the flowers in the gardens of Jun Kame and Ququb' Kame. The lords had previously told the whippoorwills, who were guardians of their gardens, "Be careful with our flowers. Don't let anyone steal them. Junajpu and Ixb'alanke will want them. Be on the alert all night!"

But the guardians were unprepared. They joyfully hung on tree branches repeating the same songs:

"Shpurpuwek, shpurpuwek!"

"Puhuyu! Puhuyu!"

In their merriment, they failed to recognize that the ants, swarming and thronging, were stealing the garden flowers, circling around the whippoorwills by climbing the trees up and down.

The ants filled four bowls. The flowers were humid with dew when the morning came.

The messengers came to get Junajpu and Ixb'alanke. "Make them bring with them our prize!"

When the twins arrived with the items that had been ordered of them, the lords became pale, their expression livid. They asked the garden guardians: "Why have you allowed the flowers to be stolen?"

"We saw nothing," they responded.

In punishment, their mouths were split open. This is the reason why the mouths of whippoorwills are wide open all day.

The ball was dropped into play again, but the game was even.

"We shall resume the game at dawn," the lords of Xibalba announced.

10

They entered the House of Cold. It is impossible to find language to describe the cold inside. The house was full of hail. It was the mansion of cold. But since Junajpu and Ixb'alanke started fires with old wood, they were healthy by sunrise.

"How is it so?" the lords of Xibalba said. They threw them into the House of Jaguars. "Devour them."

"If you don't eat us up, we will give you what you're starving for," the twins said, and they threw bones at them. The jaguars chewed on the bones and let them go by unharmed.

The lords were furious. "What kind of people are they? Where do they come from?"

Junajpu and Ixb'alanke were now put into the House of Fire, which was filled with embers, wood, and flames. But they did not burn; instead, they stoked the fire with kindling. They were healthy at sunrise again.

Desperate, the lords of Xibalba placed them in the House of Bats, which is Camazotz the vampire's place, beasts with snouts like blades that are used as deadly weapons.

The twins thought they could outmaneuver the bats by sleeping inside their blowguns. They were not bitten by the bats. One single bat, working with Camazotz, came swooping down and almost vanquished them.

All night, the bats' wings fluttered. Keeleetz! Keeleetz!" they said. At one point they were very close to one of the ends of the twins' blowguns. "Will dawn arrive soon, Junajpu?" Ixb'alanke wondered.

"Maybe it will. I will check," Junajpu answered.

Junajpu was eager to see outside the mouth of the blowgun.

"Junajpu, are you there?" Ixb'alanke wondered. "Is there light?" But Camazotz immediately cut his head off.

Ixb'alanke asked: "Is it sunrise already?" Junajpu did not move. Where is my brother? Where has Junajpu gone?" Ixb'alanke was perplexed. "What happened to him?"

Junajpu was motionless. Ixb'alanke was in despair. "Pity on us," he exclaimed. "We've been overtaken."

Everyone in Xibalba was thrilled. In no time, the lords ordered Junajpu's head to hang on the ballcourt.

11

Before daybreak, Ixb'alanke called all the animals of the night, large and small, including the *pizote* and the wild hog.

"What does each of you eat?" he asked them. "I send everyone to bring the food that belongs to you."

They went together. Some brought back rotten things. Others came with herbs. Still others returned with rocks and dust. The food of the animals was varied.

Behind them came the turtle. She arrived swaggering with her food. When she finally made it, she was carrying a chilacayote squash, which was meant to become the head of Junajpu. Eyes were carved upon it.

Numerous sages came from the sky. Heart of Heaven, Heart of Hearth, who is Juraqan, appeared over the House of Bats. Ixb'alanke began carving his brother's face in the chilacayote squash: the eyes, the hair, every one of his features. It wasn't easy but it came out well. It had become a true head. He placed it on his brother's body.

"Will he make it?" some animals wondered. "Will Junajpu return?"

"He will," others whispered. "It looks truly made of bone."

They conferred and reached an agreement: "Ixb'alanke, don't play ball with the lords of Xibalba. Just pretend you do."

"I will," he replied. He gave orders to a rabbit: "Place yourself in the middle of the tomato patch by the ballcourt. Stay there until the ball reaches you. At that point, run with it immediately. I will do the rest." The rabbit was given these instructions during the night.

Morning came. The hero twins appeared in the ballcourt. The lords were taken aback. The boys pretended as if all was fine, tossing the ball at the hoop. The rabbit grabbed the ball and scurried through the tomato patch. The lords ran after the rabbit to get the ball back.

While they were away, Ixb'alanke took possession of his brother's head. He placed it on his body. He hung the chilacayote squash where Junajpu's head had been before.

The twins were overjoyed. They went on playing for a tie.

When the lords of Xibalba returned from the tomato patch with the ball, they were surprised by what had happened.

"What is it that we see?" they exclaimed.

Upset, the two sides started to play with increased animus, scoring on equal levels.

Ixb'alanke threw a stone at the hanging squash, which fell to the ground in the middle of the ballcourt, breaking into a thousand pieces.

This is how the lords of Xibalba were defeated by Junajpu and Ixb'alanke.

12

This is the elegy of how Junajpu and Ixb'alanke died.

The hero twins summoned a pair of seers to describe their own ends. Their names were Xulu and Pakam. They told the seers: "The lords of Xibalba may inquire of you about our death, which they are orchestrating since we haven't perished yet. We suspect they will use a bonfire to bring it about. Everyone in Xibalba has agreed on this, but the truth is that we will not die. Herewith our instructions on what you must say: If you're consulted about our death, about how we should be sacrificed, what will you say, Xulu and Pakam? You must tell them that it isn't advisable because Junajpu and Ixb'alanke will resurrect. If you're asked if it would be appropriate to hang us from a tree, you should say it wouldn't be because they will have to see our faces again. And if, for the third time, you must respond if it would be good to throw our bones into the river, you should say yes, that's the right way. It would be fitting for their bones to be ground in a stone like corn flour and sprinkled over the river's waters. Let each of them be ground separately, Ixb'alanke first and Junajpu second. They will descend and ascend. The waters of the river shall disperse their remains through mountains large and small."

They bid farewell to the seers, now fully aware of their own deaths.

The lords of Xibalba proceeded to make a huge bonfire, in a type of oven, and invited the twins to drink with them.

The messengers of Jun Kame and Ququb' Kame arrived soon after.

"Go in search for the twins," they told them. "Let them come so they see what we've cooked for them. Let them witness how we straighten things out."

"Very well," they replied.

The twins were brought to the oven. The lords of Xibalba wanted to force them to play ball again with them. "Let us drink our sweet drink again," they said.

But Junajpu and Ixb'alanke knew what the plot was. "We shall not be tricked. We already know your ploy means death. We shall resist your oppression."

The twins looked at each other, spread their arms in partnership, and together jumped into the oven. They both died.

The lords were overjoyed. They celebrated by screaming and whistling. "We've defeated them! Their end has come at last!"

"Let us take our chicha and let each of us fly four times over the bonfire," Jun Kame commanded.

They called the seers, Xulu and Pakam, and asked them what to do with the bones. They said the bones should be ground and the remains should be dispersed over the river. But they didn't go far. They stayed on the surface of the water.

13

On the fifth day, the hero twins appeared again. People saw them on the water of the river. Both had the appearance of men-fish. When their faces were seen by the lords of Xibalba, they ordered a search for them.

The next day, two poor orphans showed up. They looked old and disheveled. They were dressed in rags and had a miserable aspect. The lords of Xibalba saw the orphans as they did the Dance of the Whippoorwill and the Dance of the Weasel. They also danced with Ixtzul, the centipede, and Chitic, the armadillo.

They performed many miracles, burning houses made of sticks and soon returning them to their previous state. Many in Xibalba looked at the orphans with admiration.

They then sacrificed themselves. One of them would die, inserting a dagger into his chest. Having been killed, he would immediately come back to life. Those present were incredulous.

News of the dances reached Jun Kame and Ququb' Kame. "Who are these two orphans? Do they really bring so much pleasure?" they asked.

"Their dances are truly beautiful, as is everything else they do," answered one who had brought the news.

Delighted with the portrait, the lords of Xibalba sent messengers to bring the visitors to them. To succeed, they lured them with all sorts of prizes: "Let them come here. We want to admire them and be marveled."

The messengers did as they were told, communicating the orders to the dancers.

"We don't want to," they replied. "Frankly, we are ashamed of our rags and miserable appearance. Can't you see that we are nothing but a pair of fools? What shall we tell our fellow poor who have come with us and want to see our dances and be entertained as well? We don't belong to lords."

But they were pestered, threatened with misfortune. In the end, they agreed to go because of the bribes the messengers offered them. They proceeded slowly, delaying their arrival.

When they eventually came before the lords, they were exhausted yet pretended to be surprised, even humbled by the invitation.

Asked about their homeland and their people, even their parents, they said they did not know. "Our mother and father passed away when we were little," they stated.

"Perform your tricks so we can admire you," the lords of Xibalba ordered. "We shall reward you with whatever you desire."

"We have no desire. We wish for nothing. We are only frightened by this visit."

"Don't be afraid," they were told. "Dance! Start with the part where you kill each other. Burn this house. Do every routine you know. We shall admire you, that is what our hearts want. Once you finish, we shall give you a reward for you to leave with."

As the orphans started to sing and dance, everyone in Xibalba congregated around them. They performed the Dance of the Whippoorwill and the Dance of the Weasel, and they danced with Ixtzul, the centipede, and Chitic, the armadillo.

Ququb' Kame said: "Destroy my dog and bring him back to life."

"Fine," the dancers answered. They killed the lord's dog and soon brought him back to life. The dog was truly happy, swinging his tail with enthusiasm.

Then Jun Kame said: "Burn my house to the ground." They did as he requested, burning the house of Jun Kame. The house was put back together.

The lord was stunned. "Now kill a man, sacrifice him, but let him not die."

"We are up to the challenge," the orphans again replied, as they took a man, sacrificed him, and raised up his heart to the lord's face.

Jun Kame and Ququb' Kame were dumbfounded. A minute later, the man was resuscitated, his heart palpitating normally.

In truth, the orphans were Junajpu and Ixb'alanke in disguise.

"Sacrifice yourselves now!" the lords of Xibalba ordered.

So the twins sacrificed themselves. Junajpu was killed by Ixb'alanke. His arms and legs were cut off, his head severed, his heart lifted from his chest.

The lords were speechless. Now only Ixb'alanke danced.

"Stand up," he commanded, and his sibling came back to life immediately.

Everyone was exultant.

Jun Kame and Ququb' Kame said: "Do the same with us! Sacrifice us. Destroy each one of us."

"Fine," they said as they pledged to resuscitate them after, although it wasn't their intention.

Jun Kame was killed first. Once he was gone, Ququb' Kame was put to death.

As the lords of Xibalba waited for the orphans' next move, they took leave from the place.

A sense of disbelief invaded everyone present. They began to run away quickly, finding whatever exit was closest. When they reached the canyon, they threw themselves inside it on top of each other as enormous ants arrived in great numbers and devoured them.

And then they declared their names.

14

"Listen to our names. We shall also tell you the names of our fathers. We are Junajpu and Ixb'alanke. Our fathers are those you killed, Jun Junajpu and Wuqub' Junajpu. We who are before you are the avengers of their sufferings. We suffer all the evils you caused them. Consequently, we will finish you off. None of you, the lords of Xibalba, shall escape."

The lords that were still alive fell to their knees. "Have mercy on us, Junajpu and Ixb'alanke! We sinned against your parents, who are buried in Pukbal."

"You deserve no mercy. Listen to your sentence: the ball game won't be for you anymore; your offerings will henceforth be reduced to croton sap; you'll be given only worn-out griddles and pots and other flimsy and brittle things; and only the children of weed and the desert shall speak to you. You shall know the humility of your blood."

Meanwhile, Junajpu and Ixb'alanke's grandmother cried in front of the caña her grandchildren had planted in the house. The plants had sprouted but dried up again. She waited and, happily, they sprouted again. And again. Her heart is still filled with joy as she puts candles around the plant in the form of an altar called Nikah, Center of the House. It was also called Living Maize in South Land.

And to this day too, Junajpu remains one of the twenty named days of the K'iche' calendar. We build altars decorated with incense, food, and flowers to his memory.

Unfortunately, the lords of Xibalba rebounded.

Part III: Sunrise

1

Now hear how humans were made and how their journey ended in catastrophe. Their appearance is linked to the sunrise.

A number of separate creations had been attempted: the mountains and rivers, the animals and birds, and the wooden people. Tepew and Q'uq'umatz, the Creator and Maker, said: "The time is ripe for us to conclude the work we started, which shall sustain and nurture us. It is proper for the clarified children, the civilized vassals, to appear now and for humanity to spread over the face of the earth."

They reflected and discussed in the darkness of night. From Paxil, meaning broken, split, or cleft, and Cayala, meaning bitter or stagnant water, yellow and white corn was used to create humans. That is why the K'iche' people are rooted in maize whereas foreigners who eat bread are wheat people. To be a *qas winaq*, a true person, one must eat maize. From it, language will come.

The animals who discovered this food are Yak the fox, Utiw the coyote, Kel the parakeet. They showed the way to Paxil and Cayala. The food then entered the flesh of humans. From it human blood was made. That is how maize became part of humans.

Tepew and Q'uq'umatz were happy to have settled in a beautiful land, full of delight, abundant in yellow and white corn, fruits and seeds, including beans, cacao, *zapote*, *anonas* [custard apple], jocotes, matasanos, and honey. All the necessary food was available.

Along with water granting strength, food entered the flesh, for humans are distinguished from wooden people in having blood coursing like rivers inside their bodies. They also have a soul, which is a ghost connected with the body at birth that communes with the body in unpredictable ways.

Thereafter, Tepew and Q'uq'umatz were in conversation about the creation of our first mother and our first father. From white and yellow corn, their flesh was made. And from them, four humans came about. They were the progenitors.

2

These are the names of the first humans that were created: the first was Balam Kitze; the second, Balam Aqab; the third, Majukutaj; and the fourth, Iq Balam. They contained in their blood the divine sight.

They had no navel since they were not born from woman. Nor were they shaped by Tepew and Q'uq'umatz in any deliberate fashion. Instead, they came about miraculously and by chance. Still, they were human in that they could talk, see, hear, walk, and grasp objects, handsome males endowed with intelligence. And as they appreciated the vault of Heaven and the roundness of Earth, the four were capable of understanding the limits of their condition. But they could also easily become infatuated with their own power.

After the Creator and Maker, who didn't appreciate the pride exhibited by the humans, asked them what they thought of their state, the four humans were instantly grateful. "We're thankful to the Creator and Maker.

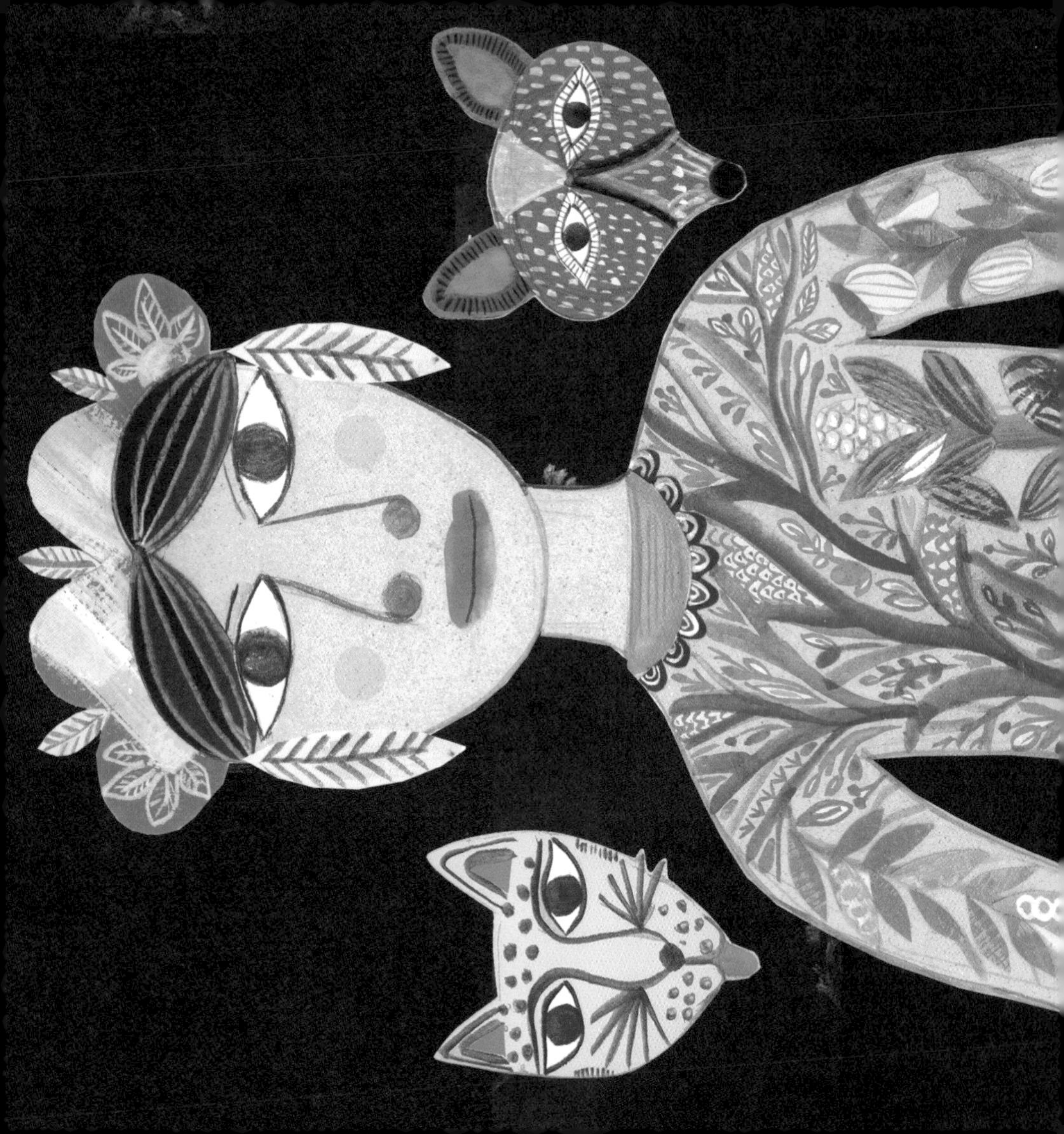

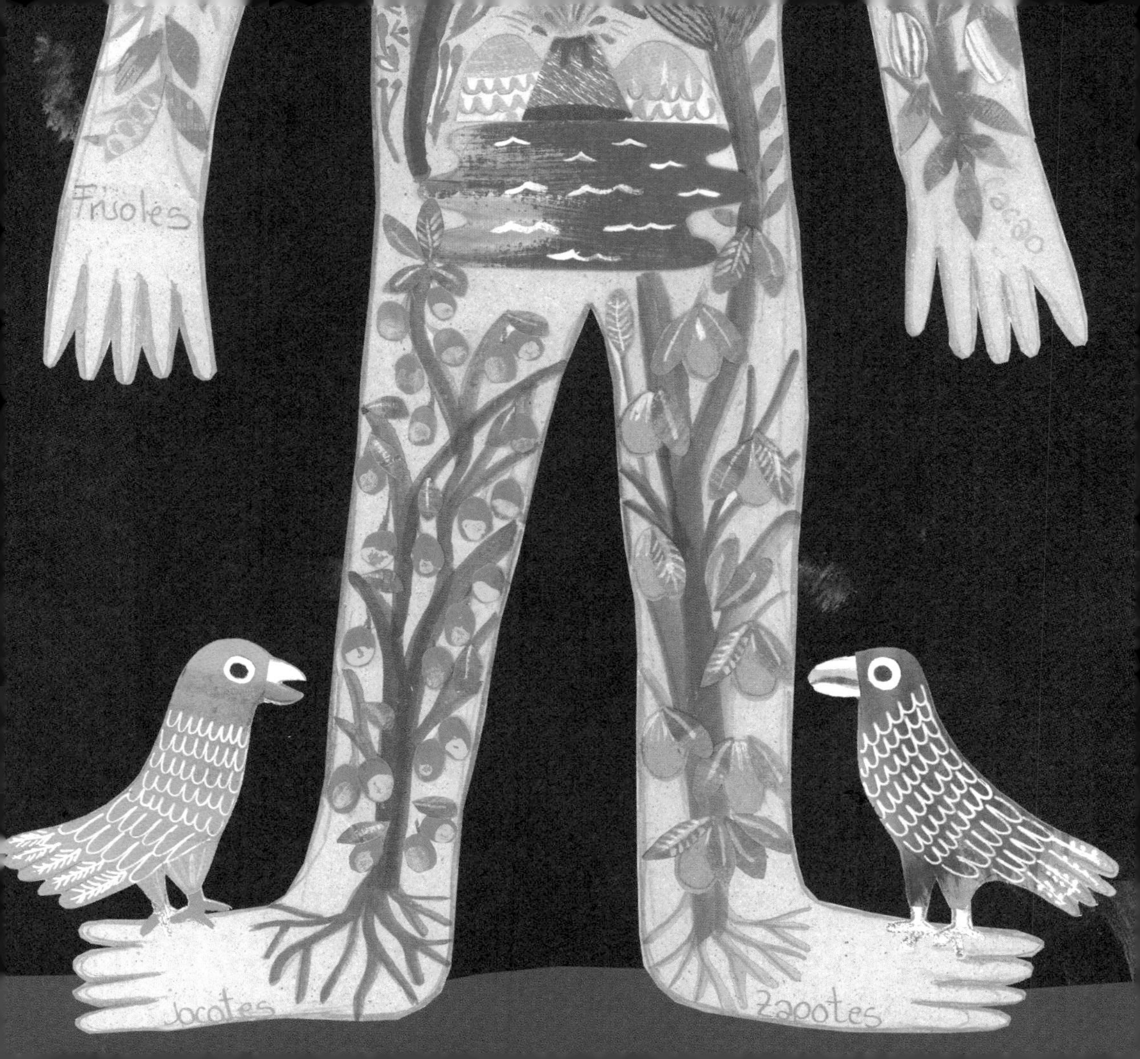
Frijoles
cacao
Jocotes
zapotes

We've learned everything, great and small. We have been given senses and are able to feel. We know what is near and far, and small and large in Heaven and Earth."

Soon after, their female companions were created because only a married person is considered complete. They arrived in a dream, endowed with true knowledge. When the four males woke up, the couples were immediately filled with happiness.

These are the names of the four wives: Kaja Paluna, Chomija, Tzununija, and Kaquixaja. Along with the four males, they multiplied, engendering all the tribes of the K'iche' people.

Balam Kitze was the grandfather and the father of the nine big houses of the Kawek. Balam Aqab, the grandfather and father of the nine large houses of the Najaib. Majukutaj, the grandfather and father of the four big houses of the Ajaw K'iche'.

Humans multiplied in the East. They were black humans and white humans and humans of other varieties. Some lived in the forest and had no houses.

Praising Heart of Heaven, Heart of Earth, everyone congregated at sunrise: "Let our people be plentiful. Let them find joy and not fear. Let them live in peace instead of war."

But there was no response. The gods were disappointed with human actions on Earth. There was much deceit, much competition, much violence. To show their displeasure, sunrise was delayed.

3

Heart of Heaven, Heart of Earth was unhappy. “It is wrong what our creatures say,” Tepew and Q’uq’umatz confessed. “What shall we do with them? Their sight should reach only what is in their purview; they should be able to see only a fraction of what is worthwhile on the face of the earth. But are they not by nature creatures made in our semblance? Might they want to be gods? What if they do not procreate? What if they don’t spread over the face of the earth?”

The Creator and Maker added: “It isn’t good what they said: ‘We’ve learned everything, great and small.’ Let us put a stop to their desires, for it is not good what we see in the humans. Might they feel equal to us, their creators, who are able to contemplate enormous distances, who can know everything at every time from numerous perspectives?”

Heart of Heaven, Heart of Earth decided to change the nature of creation.

A mist was spread over human sight, making it murky like the reflection of the moon over a mirror. Judgment was compromised.

This didn't become clear to the K'iche' people until the progenitors took advantage of them.

4

The progenitors—Balam Kitze, Balam Aqab, Majukutaj, and Iq Balam—waited for sunrise until they lost patience.

They said: "Heart of Heaven, Heart of Earth doesn't want us. Let us search for idols that might protect us. Where we find ourselves now we have no defenders." They added: "That will justify us, granting us order." They heard news of a citadel toward which many traveled. The place was known as Tulan Suiwa, in the highlands of Guatemala.

Several idols quickly emerged to replace Heart of Heaven, Heart of Earth for the K'iche' people. The first was Tojil, which means payment, debt, obligation, or tribute, but also thunder. Tojil was shown to the people by Balam Kitze inside a pack frame that contained him.

Then came Awilix, who was brought by Balam Aqab and sometimes appears as a young man. The god known as Jakavitz was presented by Majukutaj.

Heart of Heaven

Heart of Earth

And the god Nikatakaj was brought out by Iq Balam. These idols were arrogant. They fashioned themselves as tormentors, dispensing threats.

"We have finally found what we've been looking for," the progenitors announced to the K'iche' people.

Even though everyone among the K'iche' people was poor, their determination was strong. Still, as soon as they arrived at Tulan Suiwa it became clear that the Rabinales, the Kaqchikeles, the Aj Tzikinaja, and other tribes, including the Yaqui, all of whom had been conquered at war, spoke different languages, meaning they could not come together as a single nation.

"Ay," the K'iche' people said. "We've gained protection but lost the capacity to connect with ourselves. Have we been deceived?"

5

They had no fire. Only the followers of Tojil had it.

"Ay, we will die of cold." Tojil answered: "I am your god." Soon a rainstorm descended on all, along with an abundance of hail. The fire was extinguished.

Other tribes that had been captured in wars by the K'iche' people were cold as well. They asked for help: "Have compassion on us. Wasn't our homeland once one and the same, when we were created?"

In truth, they were scheming a subversion. A messenger with bat-like wings came from Xibalba: "Tojil is the representation of the memory of your Creator and Maker. Do not give fire to other people until they give offerings to Tojil. Ask Tojil what it is you should give them."

They did as they were told and every tribe considering revolt acquiesced.

Only one tribe refused to bow down: the Kaqchikeles, who were from the house of Tzotzil. Their idol was called Chamalkan, represented by a bat.

They organized a movement to resist the control of the K'iche' people. They used arrows and stones. Their plot was simple: when the K'iche' people were bowing down to Tojil, they surrounded them.

But the K'iche' people did not fall. They killed many Kaqchikeles. Others ran away and formed another kingdom, which lived in freedom until they were subjugated by Pedro de Alvarado.

They are sometimes called Cakchiquel, Cakchiquel, Kakchiquel, Caqchikel, and Cachiquel. Their language is still spoken today. They occasionally helped the bearded white man. Their capital was in the ruins of Mixco Viejo, near Chimaltenango.

6

In Tulan Suiwa, it was customary to fast while awaiting the sunrise. The K'iche' people took turns looking at the great star called Ikoquih that arrives, always brilliant, before the sun.

But Ikoquih did not appear. The K'iche' people abandoned Tulan Suiwa, moving East. "This is not our house," Tojil said to them. "Let us go where we will settle down." Tojil spoke to Balam Kitze, Balam Aqab, Majukutaj, and Iq Balam. They announced: "Leave behind your good deeds. Take whatever is necessary to bleed our ears, and make your sacrifices. That shall be your gratitude toward god."

They allowed blood to spurt from their ears. And in their chants they cried for the departure from Tulan Suiwa.

"Ay, our hearts are in pain because we shall not see the sunrise anymore in this land," they said as they departed.

They left behind only a few of their people to preserve their memory.

7

They reached the top of a mountain. All the people who comprise the K'iche' nation except the Kaqchikeles came together there. They sought advice to reach decisions. That mountain is now called Chi Pixab.

"We are the K'iche' people. You shall be Tamub. And you, Ilokab, this will be your name. And these three K'iche' people, they shall not disappear, for they have a common fate."

They also gave a name to the Rabinales, who kept their name, which has not been lost ever since. And likewise to the Tzikinaja, also still called this name.

They all gathered together to await the sunrise and to observe the arrival of Ikoquih. "We are wandering people," they said.

They were starving.

But Ikoquih didn't appear.

It isn't known how they crossed the sea to return to their origin, only that they walked on stones that formed paths on the surface of the water. They called these Row of Stones and also Teared Sand.

They congregated in the mountain called Chi Pixab. They had taken Tojil with them. Balam Kitze was with his wife, Kaja Paluna, and Balam Aqab with his wife, Chomija. Majukutaj observed an absolute fast with his wife, Tzununija. And Iq Balam was with his wife, Kaquixaja.

The progenitors fasted in the darkness of night.

8

Tojil, Awilix, and Jakavitz spoke to the progenitors: "We must arise. Dawn is approaching. Put us in hiding. It would be disgraceful if we were imprisoned by our enemies within these walls. Make for us a place worthy of us."

"We shall march on," the progenitors responded. "We'll go in search of the forests."

Each of them took responsibility for his own god. That's how they took Awilix to Euabal Ivan, the great canyon of the forest we now call Pa Awilix. Balam Aqab left him there.

The rest they left as well. Jakavitz was left on a red pyramid, on the hill now known as Hacavitz.

Majukutaj stayed with his own god.

Then came Balam Kitze, who went to a hill in the forest where he hid

Tojil. Snakes, jaguars, rattlesnakes, and pit vipers crowded the place. The hill is now known as Pa Tojil.

But night after night, the progenitors couldn't sleep. The anxiety in their hearts was enormous. They knew their end was near. Heart of Heaven, Heart of Earth had commanded them to lead the K'iche' people. But they were more interested in themselves. Perhaps that's why, although they were made of white and yellow corn, Balam Kitze, Balam Aqab, Majukutaj, and Iq Balam had no navel.

A poor leader is one who becomes indulgent.

It was clear to them, their idols, and the K'iche' people that sunrise would not come.

Part IV: Promise

1

Destruction has taken hold. It came about when our own leaders turned against us. This tragedy unfolded for a long time. Nobody was fully aware until it was too late.

It started when the progenitors—Balam Kitze, Balam Aqab, Majukutaj, and Iq Balam—pretended to be demigods. Whenever a person would pass by the roads, they would immediately behave as if they were coyotes and wildcats. They imitated the sounds of pumas and jaguars.

"They want to pretend they are not human, to trick us all," the people said. "This in their hearts. They want to get rid of us."

The truth is, the progenitors were restless. They would arrive at their houses with their wives by their side, carrying with them the offspring of wasps, bees, and bumblebees. Although their wives would be satisfied with these offerings, it was a sign that their connection to the people was tense. An incipient form of resistance was palpable.

Then the progenitors arrived before Tojil, Awilix, and Jakavitz. They asked to be treated differently.

A transformation was underway. The progenitors would prick their ears and arms before the idols, collecting the blood and placing it in a vase, near the stone. But in truth they weren't made of stone. Each of them appeared in the figure of a boy.

The progenitors were insatiable for blood and wanted more: "We seek new forms of strength and vigor." They began to ask for offerings themselves. "If you follow our commands, your salvation shall be near!" the progenitors told the people.

2

Soon they turned against those whom the K'iche' had captured in wars. The tribes of Vuk Amag were soon massacred, even though they were innocent.

They kidnapped men as they were walking, and soon they sacrificed them before Tojil and Awilix, their blood spread on the road, their heads put on display. When the people asked what happened, the progenitors lied. "The jaguar ate them," they said.

The tribes didn't realize the scope of the tragedy until it was too late. They started doubting their deities: "Might it be the fault of Tojil and Awilix?" Eventually, they focused on the progenitors. "They pretend to be connected to our noblemen. Where might their houses be?"

They discussed it together, then started to follow the clues. They could only detect footprints of beasts and jaguars. The first footprints were inverted and difficult to follow, and their path wasn't clear. A fog rolled in, a black rain came down, and there was much mud. A drizzle followed. This is what the people saw among themselves. And their hearts were tired of looking because Tojil, Awilix, and Jakavitz were very large. They went far to the top of the mountains, in the vicinity of the villages, where they killed people.

By now, Tojil, Awilix, and Jakavitz had the appearance of three young men. They walked virtuously and consulted a magical stone.

There was a river where they bathed. It was called The Bath of Tojil. "How might we defeat them?" As soon as someone saw them, they would disappear.

News of sightings of the progenitors spread. The noblemen deliberated among themselves, requesting everyone to help: "Not one of us should be left behind. If we must perish as a result of these kidnappings, let it be so. Tojil, Awilix, and Jakavitz are strong. It's impossible for them to defeat us. Are not there enough of us? The K'iche' of Kawek are not many."

They decided on a strategy that had already been used successfully in the past: "Let us send beautiful maidens to meet them. The progenitors will be taken by desire."

A group of maidens was chosen. They were given instructions: "Go, daughters. Wash the clothes in the river. If you see three young men, undress before them. When you notice them overwhelmed by desire, tell them you are daughters of noblemen."

They added: "Take off your clothes. And if afterward they want to kiss you, give yourselves to them. If you do not, we will kill you. When you have their clothes in your control, bring them here as proof of your actions."

Ixtah and Ixpuch were their names. Their courage was unparalleled. The maidens were sent to the river where Tojil, Awilix, and Jakavitz bathed. They were dressed in their best outfits when they left.

As soon as they reached the river, Ixtah and Ixpuch started to wash. They got undressed and were next to the rocks when Tojil, Awilix, and Jakavitz arrived. They were surprised by the maidens but felt no desire. The idols asked them: "Where do you come from? What are you looking for in coming to the edge of the river?"

"We've been sent by the noblemen," the maidens answered. "We were told to go see Tojil's face and bring proof of it."

Tojil, Awilix, and Jakavitz said to them: "Wait a moment and you'll be given the proof you require."

Tojil told Balam Kitze, Balam Aqab, and Majukutaj to paint four capes for the maidens. Iq Balam didn't paint a cape. On Balam Kitze's cape, Tojil painted a jaguar. Balam Aqab drew an eagle on his and Majukutaj, wasps and horseflies. The capes were then taken to the maidens in the river. "Here is proof that you talked to Tojil. Take these capes to the noblemen of the tribes so that they may wear them."

Ixtah and Ixpuch went back with the capes. When they arrived, the tribes' noblemen were full of happiness.

"Did you see Tojil's face?"

"Yes," Ixtah and Ixpuch replied.

"Do you have proof?"

The maidens extended the painted capes covered in jaguars, eagles, wasps, and horseflies. They noblemen immediately felt the need to wear them.

The jaguar did nothing when the first nobleman placed the cape on his back. A second nobleman put on a cape with the drawing of an eagle, and felt fine beneath it. They showed them off to everyone. Then a third nobleman took off his clothes and placed the cape with wasps and horseflies over his shoulders. At that moment, the wasps and horseflies began to bite them all. Unable to tolerate the pain, the noblemen started to scream.

Soon after, they asked Ixtah and Ixpuch: "What type of capes did you bring back?"

Eventually, they said: "The people have been subjugated by Tojil. Our gods no longer represent us. The time has come to revolt."

3

The tribes again gathered in council: "What shall we do? Our progenitors have become traitors. They are powerful and might undermine any of our efforts. We must kill them with shields and archers. Are we not many? The majority will rule. Nobody among us should be left behind." They thus spoke. And all the people took up weapons. The number of enemies ready to kill had by now become substantial.

The subversion began. The progenitors gathered on a hill named Jakavitz. Its top is rather small. The tribes decided to kill them when they were all together. People were loaded with weapons. Everyone followed orders.

"They will be destroyed. We shall take Tojil as prisoner."

However, Tojil knew everything and so did Balam Kitze, Balam Aqab, and Majukutaj, since they could find no rest as a result of their anxiety.

The warriors crested the hill. But they were tired because they hadn't slept the night before. Soon their eyebrows and beards were cut off, their metal

ornaments, crowns, and necklaces taken away. This was done to punish and humiliate them.

As soon as they woke up, they all wanted to recover their crowns and sticks but they could not. "Who has stripped us of our weapons? Who has shaved our beards? Are these demons who steal our men? They shall not succeed in making us afraid. We shall conquer enemy cities by force. That is how we will see our silver again. This is what we shall do."

The progenitors' hearts were stubborn. They built a wall on the edges of the city and fenced it. They created dummies that looked like humans, making them stand on a line next to the wall. They equipped them with shields and arrows and adorned them with metal crowns.

They also dug cavernous holes around the city. They asked for advice from Tojil: "Will they defeat us? Will we end up dead?"

Tojil was now against the people, too. "I'm here next to you," Tojil told the progenitors. "Don't be afraid!"

They went off to catch wasps and horseflies, which they placed in four huge pots to combat the people. They placed the pots around the fortress wall. Then they hid themselves.

There were spies for the tribes, strategically located around the fortress wall. But they saw only mannequins softly moving their shields and arches. These mannequins resembled soldiers. The spies sighed in relief when they realized the mannequins were few.

The tribes, in comparison, were plentiful, made of brave warriors.

4

The progenitors were together on the mountain, along with their wives and children, when the warriors arrived.

Armed with shields and arrows, the tribes surrounded the fortress around the city, banging their drums. They whistled, screamed, and shouted energetically, inciting war.

The noblemen saw the progenitors and their idols from the edge of the wall, where they were with their women and children. Fortunately, they weren't intimidated. They assembled their armies in an orderly fashion.

It was time to lay siege to the city when the four huge pots were opened, a curtain of wasps and horseflies emerging from them. The warriors were stung everywhere.

"How did these insects get here?"

The wasps and horseflies buzzed furiously, overwhelming the warriors, who were unable to use their weapons, bending to the ground instead. They lay on the ground, in great pain, and did not feel the axes of Balam Kitze and Balam Aqab as they struck them. The progenitors' wives also came to kill. Hundreds perished. The first ones to arrive were also the first to die.

Courage turned into suffering.

Humiliated, the tribes surrendered. "Have mercy on us," they said. "Don't kill us."

"You shall become our servants," the progenitors told them.

This is how the tribes were defeated by our first mothers and fathers. It happened in Jakavitz, which is where they first became the K'iche' people, where they multiplied, their daughters becoming pregnant, their children born.

5

The treacherous progenitors—Balam Kitze, Balam Aqab, Majukutaj, and Iq Balam—finally died. Their demise allowed a respite for the K'iche' people.

The *Popol Vuh* is meant to establish the various lineages, for it is important to remember who belongs to which house. The bearded white man is intent on dismantling our traditions. After his arrival, ball playing fell into disuse. We must resist by keeping track of who we are and where we originated.

Aware of their end, the progenitors found time to advise their children. At the time, they were not sick, nor were they in agony.

These are the names of their sons: Balam Kitze, who was the grandfather and father of those in Kavek, had two sons: Kokawib and Kokabib.

Balam Aqab from Nahib also had these sons: Kuakul and Koakutek.

Majukutaj had only one son: Kuajaw.

Iq Balam had no children.

Majukutaj
Balam Kitze

Balam Agab
Iq Balam

The progenitors said goodbye to them. Together, the four started to sing, their hearts overwhelmed by sadness. There was warmth in their hearts when they sang the Kamuku.

"Oh, children! We are prepared to leave but we will give you wise advice and healthy recommendations. And to you, our wives, you should visit our faraway homeland. The return is essential. Everything that goes up must come down and everything that starts must end too. These are the cycles of life. You must return to our origin, the homeland we left behind in the East. It is ours forever and it shall be where you settle down. The forces of nature are intangible. Our Lord of Deer is in its right place. We've fulfilled our mission. Think of us! Do not erase us from your memory. You shall return to your homes and your mountains by continuing on your paths."

They thus spoke as they said goodbye. Balam Kitze gave a signal.

They were not buried by their women, nor by their children, since they disappeared leaving no trace. Incense was burned.

The people remembered them thereafter. The progenitors were enwrapped in the sheet of memory. It is called the Wrapping of Greatness. They were the first men from the other side of the sea, where the sun is born.

The wives of Balam Kitze, Balam Aqab, and Majukutaj also died in the mountains. Their treasonous campaign had come to an end.

6

Afterward, the descendants of the progenitors, called Kokabib, Koakutek, and Kuajaw, decided to go East, hoping to fulfill the wish of the ancestors, whom they had not forgotten. This happened a long time after the progenitors died.

As they departed, the three said: "Let's go to the land of our origins."

None of them were vain. They were intelligent and experienced. They said goodbye to their families and relatives and departed happily. "We shall not die, we will return," they said.

They crossed the sea to reach the East. They received banners from the lord of the place, Nakxit, King of the East, as well as from Ahpop Kamja and Ahpop, also members of royalty. They gave them banners, a throne, flutes, puma and jaguar claws, deer heads and legs, snail shells, tobacco, zucchini, papagayo feathers, Tatam and Caxon. They brought all these items to Tulan Suiwa.

Having reached the town called Jakavitz, the tribes of Tamub and Hokab came together to greet Kokabib, Koakutek, and Kuajaw, who took over the government.

The ones from Rabinal were joyful, as were the Kaqchikeles and the Aj Tzikinaja, sharing banners and other insignias.

Soon the survivors left Jakavitz, looking for other places to settle and build new cities, which is how they founded the city of Chi Ismachi, where they lived in peace and multiplied, giving away their daughters in exchange for presents, which was a custom that drew benefits. As soon as three other nations, Kawek, Najaib, and Ilokab, joined them, the K'iche' ruled over other tribes. They searched for their wives from among them.

After abandoning Chi Ismachi, they came to another place, where they founded the ancient capital city of Q'umarkaj, now known as Santa Cruz del K'iche'. There they split again, building new cities: Chi Kix, Chichak, Humetaja, Kulba, and Kavinal. Since they were numerous, they had looked for other places to settle.

Migration is a form of punishment. The original K'iche' who had gone East had already died. They didn't get used to the different places they crossed to, suffering hardship. They longed for home, as do our descendants who, in moving North today, forget their roots.

7

Those who migrated developed their power in the beautiful city called Izmaki, building structures made of mortar under the fourth generation of kings.

Konake and Belejeb Queh governed. Then came King Kotuja and Iztayul, also known as Ahpop and Ahpop Kamja, who reigned in Izmaki. It was a city known for its colorful birds. It was said to contain a feather of every bird ever created by Heart of Heaven, Heart of Earth.

Only three dynasties existed in Izmaki. One was Kavek, another was Najaib, and the third was Ahau K'iche'. Only two had successors, the branches of the K'iche' and Tamub.

They were all together in Izmaki—with a single thought, without fights, at peace, with neither envy nor jealousy. Its greatness was limited, though: they deliberately did not want to expand.

Seeing this, those from Ilokab started a war. They wanted to kill the king of Kotuja, hoping to have a single chief. With regard to King Iztayul, they sought to punish him. But King Kotuja died from illness before they could kill him.

It was the beginning of a revolt that led to war. What they wanted was the ruin of the K'iche' people, hoping to reign themselves. But they arrived only to die. They were captured. Their captivity lasted a long time. Not many escaped.

Soon there began to be human sacrifices. Those from Ilokab were sacrificed in punishment for their sins, according to an order by King Kotuja. Many more were enslaved who had sought the demise of the K'iche' people.

At this point, the K'iche' empire was truly large. A visitor once described its confines as "large enough for the sun never to set." In every sense, they had prodigious kings. No one could dominate them. There was no one who could humiliate the city of Izmaki.

Large and small, every tribe that witnessed the arrival of the captives was fearful. The captives were sacrificed by order of King Kotuja and King Iztayul, whose people were the Najaib and Ahau K'iche'.

Only three branches of the K'iche' family were in Izmaki. Orgies around their daughters began when they were asked to be married. The three dynasties were thereafter joined together, eating and drinking.

"This is how we show gratitude. This is how we open the path to our posterity," their fathers said. "Let us be united, we of Kavek, Najaib, and Ahau K'iche'."

They stayed in Izmaki for a long time.

8

They arrived at the city of Kumarkaaj, a name given by King Q'uq'umatz. The fifth generation of humans had thus begun.

Splendor came when the House of God was revealed. It was built by prisoners of war. The growth of the empire followed.

This was the time when the power of the K'iche' people truly evolved. It was thanks to the above-mentioned King Q'uq'umatz, who was the greatest leader our nation has ever known. Under him, our children built houses in ravines, creating splendid cities.

As is well known, King Q'uq'umatz is named after one of the parts of the Creator and Maker. The other part is Tepew. He was born enlightened, with a drawing of corn on the back of his head. His eyes were green, his air undulated like seawater. Since he was young, he meditated while he fasted. He never uttered a word without first pondering it. He could draw. He also was sharp with numbers.

Ahpop

Ahpop Kamja

Under his reign, there was no theft or violence. People came together to listen to the advice of the king. There was order based on mutual affection. This prevented war. The K'iche' people never lived in better times. Unfortunately, his reign did not last long.

King Q'uq'umatz was truly prodigious. He was known as a poet, a musician, and an adroit ballplayer. He ascended to Heaven for seven days and another seven days he descended to Xibalba. For seven days he became a serpent. For another seven days he became an eagle. And, for another seven days, he was a jaguar too. His appearance was that of these animals during those periods. During another seven days he became coagulated blood.

News of his magic spread quickly and other kings felt terror toward King Q'uq'umatz. He also was disguised as Ahpop and Ahpop Kamja.

9

Then came the bearded white men, tall and defiant, on horses, with booming guns. They arrived from the sea.

Nobody among the K'iche' people was aware of their arrival, although King Q'uq'umatz had prophesized the end of time since it was originally made by means of water in the rivers created by Heart of Heaven, Heart of Earth.

"There will be blood running through the rivers. Mothers and fathers, sisters and brothers shall perish. Sunset shall overtake the people," King Q'uq'umatz said after reading the *Popol Vuh*. "The age of silence shall reign. This will happen after two great kings, Quicab of the House of Cavec, and Cavizimah of the house of Achac-Iboy. Dispersion will follow."

This happened in Chulimal.

At first, the silhouettes of the bearded white men fulgurated, the way the profiles of ominous deities do. Their power was beyond light, though.

Ailments spread among the K'iche'. People died of fever, coughing, and diarrhea.

"The only way for the K'iche' people to survive is to inhabit Xibalba without letting themselves be overwhelmed by its lords," King Q'uq'umatz announced.

Such a pronouncement was perplexing. Xibalba is where the twins Junajpu and Ixb'alanke defeated evil. That was no small feat. "The people are weak," the priests said. "They will perish without much resistance."

King Q'uq'umatz appealed to Heart of Heaven, Heart of Earth: "Let there be promise! Juraqan, giver of wealth! Giver of daughters and sons! Turn your glories and wealth in our direction. Grant my children and followers life. Let them multiply and grow, those who invoke you on the road, in the fields, on the edge of the river, in the canyons, under the trees, and along the cornfield."

He continued: "Let the K'iche' people arrive at the sunrise they deserve. Grant them daughters and sons! Let them not be met by disgrace and misfortune. Let the deceiver, the bearded white man, not approach them, either before or behind them. Let them not fall. Let them not be wounded. Let them not fornicate. Let them not be condemned by justice. Let them not fall on the road. Let them not encounter obstacles either before or behind them, nor anything that hits them. Let them defeat the bearded white man's sorcery."

Thus spoke our leader, King Q'uq'umatz, who began to fast, as an admonition against the approaching darkness.

One morning, after he fasted for seven days and nights, the benevolent king announced that, in exchange for future prosperity, he had been summoned by the lords of Xibalba.

Unfortunately, his adventures in the underworld are not known to the K'iche' people, although it is believed he might be playing ball with Jun Kame and Ququb' Kame.

10

The bearded white men intermingled with K'iche' women. They impregnated them. Soon, they conquered fields and cities, small and large villages, all of which paid heavily. The priests suggested that people bring precious stones and metals as offerings. They also brought bee honey, emerald bracelets, and blue feathers.

Sunset was nigh.

One day, a healer who lived among the white, bearded men, called Father Francisco Ximénez, approached a pair of twin girls. Their names were Kikab and Kavizimaj. They were bright. In their exchange, the twins told Father Ximénez about the ancient book, *Popol Vuh*. They said an actual copy was in the possession of King Q'uq'umatz, but he preferred it to vanish instead of allowing it to fall into the hands of the bearded white men.

"It was surrounded by flames," Kikab and Kavizimaj said. "It is collected in our minds. We know every sound in it, every image. We know what's right and what's wrong in its pages."

Father Ximénez had taught the twin girls how to dress. Listening to their anecdotes about the *Popol Vuh*, he was perplexed. He asked the twin girls to recite the beginning.

They said: "In the beginning, everything is placid. The womb of the sky is empty. Everything is still. Time has not yet begun. There are no humans. Nor is there bird, fish, crab, tree, stone, hollow, canyon, meadow, or forest. Only the sky exists, as well as water, which is in repose."

In the nights that followed, Father Ximénez heard longer segments. He asked the parents of the twin girls for permission for K'iche' scribes to write down their anecdotes in the K'iche' language using the Latin alphabet. For us, to write (*dzib*) also means to paint and draw, by which I want to make clear that these stories are visual. He then translated the stories into Castilian. But he didn't publish it alone. Instead, he released two works: first, a grammatical treatise of the Kaqchikel, K'iche', and Tz'utujil languages, and second, a manual for Catholic priests to administer the sacraments and confessions. The *Popol Vuh* was appended to the second treatise.

Short, well-rounded, with bronze skin, dark, greasy hair and a stern look, Father Ximénez was a humble, learned man, but his intentions were suspicious. He didn't compile the stories for the betterment of our people. Instead, as he himself stated, he wanted them to be used to persuade the K'iche' to follow the Christian faith in the fight against the devil, "just like

Popol-Vuh
Ilan Stavans
Gabriela Larios

military commanders against their enemies." He wrote: "This is the aim of the second treatise that contains a confessionary and a catechism. I also added another treatise that I translated from K'iche' into Castilian. Here can be seen the errors with which Satan attempts to wage war on these miserable Indians."

Father Ximénez wanted to satisfy the curiosity of many who saw the condition of our people. What were their beliefs? Did they pray to Jesus Christ? Were they truly human, or were they apes? There still is considerable debate over these lies.

It should be known that the *Popol Vuh* wasn't revealed only to Father Ximénez, but to other Dominican friars as well. Yet he had a particular portal into our world. While serving as parish priest in the K'iche' town of Chichicastenango, he learned of the many books we kept and how we memorized them to transport them without peril.

We are not the devil. Instead, we have lived under oppression. Our women have been raped. Our children have been taken away from us. Disease has spread among us. Those of us who remain are vulnerable.

Living in fear often means talking in secret, keeping our thoughts from being heard. It's a miserable time. Yet oppression also fortifies the soul. We've learned to be stronger, savvier, more decisive in what we do.

Coda

In this cave, away from any distraction, I speak to you, daughters of Kikab. You must persevere. Your intelligence permeates your actions. Your magic may equal that of your ancestors whose name you carry. Your turn has come. One of you has jaguar skin, the other leopard spots.

I am a *curandera*, a healer. I'm fifty-seven years old. I was born in Chichicastenango and have lived in Chiapas, Yucatán, and Quintana Roo. I have six children. I never fully learned the K'iche' alphabet; I only know how to read the Latin alphabet.

Fake leaders have betrayed us. They have forced idols on us to eclipse our true deities. Remember that in our stories, the younger sibling is the one endowed with continuity, prevailing in most ordeals, while the older sibling is punished for the courage they both project.

It is my duty to pass on the memory I received from my mother, as she did from her own mother, and so on. There is danger all around us.

The world created by Heart of Heaven, Heart of Earth is dying. The birds, the serpents, the rattlesnakes, the bumblebees are all furious. They realize their homes are vanishing. The rivers are drying up. Juraqan, whose power shakes nature, has no mercy.

Xibalba is about to become visible.

The progenitors brought despair to our people. They were a failed creation. King Q'uq'umatz foresaw the future but lacked the power to set us on the right path. House divisions have forced us to abandon our lands. Communing with maize is no longer a priority. Xibalba is now everywhere.

The essence of the K'iche' people is now in danger, our memory in peril. Sing the poetry of Ixkik'. There is promise and with it, sunrise.

Might there be another chance for us? Might our people reconvene from the diasporas we now inhabit?

Listen to me!

Retelling the Tale

I first encountered the *Popol Vuh* in the 1970s, when I was a teenager in Mexico. I read it alongside the less fanciful, more severe *Legends of Guatemala* (1930), by Guatemala's Nobel Prize winner Miguel Ángel Asturias. These books were a window into the Maya population I regularly mingled with.

Xibalba, the underworld, which commands Part II of the *Popol Vuh*, was especially alluring to me in the way that Gehena in the *Talmud* and Purgatory in Dante's *Divine Comedy* were. I imagined it as a concealed universe designed by someone with Italo Calvino's ingenuity.

A decade later, I delved deeper into the world of the Maya—not only the *Popol Vuh* but also its sibling *The Books of Chilam Balam*—after I met Miguel León-Portilla (1926–2019), the illustrious scholar of pre-Columbian civilizations. His *Seven Essays about Nahuatl Culture* (1958) was life-changing, allowing me to appreciate wholeheartedly the philosophical sophistication of indigenous thought. The aboriginal population of the region known as Mesoamerica is still ostracized, and it was even more so at the time, when a revival of indigenous cultures was beginning to take shape in political, religious, literary, culinary, and artistic realms. León-Portilla's volume was the engine behind it.

Almost as invaluable, years later, was his summa *In the Language of Kings: An Anthology of Mesoamerican Literature: Pre-Columbian to the Present* (2001). Through it, I became conscious of the extent to which, although rooted in the highlands of Guatemala, the *Popol Vuh* belongs to humankind. Making it ours—that is, endorsing its universality—doesn't take it away from the K'iche' people; on the contrary, it strengthens its local roots.

As with the Bible, *Gilgamesh*, the *Iliad* and *Odyssey*, and other ancient books, the shaping of this collection of sacred K'iche' tales started through oral tradition. It was written down after the Spanish conquest, sometime in the middle of the sixteenth century, in part as a rescue effort after the devastation the indigenous community had experienced at the hands of the Europeans. The travel from the spoken to the printed word is, needless to say, treacherous. So much was lost in the process.

Interestingly, given the dozens of translations, adaptations, and appropriations the *Popol Vuh* has fostered since then, its refashioning is as alive today as it was before it became a physical book. Like speakers, translators are never innocent. Objective as they purport to be, they invariably add and take away based on an overt or unconscious agenda.

The *Popol Vuh* is also alive in countless adaptations, from videos to children's stories to theater and musical versions, including Argentine composer Alberto Ginastera's inspired symphonic poem in seven movements, written between 1975 and 1983.

My own desire to retell the tale of the fearless twins Junajpu and Ixb'alanke and their descendants came serendipitously. I was performing my one-man play *The Oven* (2018), about a shamanic ceremony in the Colombian Amazon that included the ingestion of the hallucinogenic ayahuasca. The endeavor reconnected me with my own indigenous past in Mexico. The show's director, Matthew Glassman, was concerned about the play's appropriation of aboriginal culture. Our spirited debate opened my eyes. My response was to delve deeper into the world of Nahuatl, Maya, and K'iche' civilizations.

At some point during the performances I was on a trip to Oxford, United Kingdom, when I stumbled upon a copy of Charles and Mary Lamb's *Tales from Shakespeare* (1907). I always loved what the Lamb siblings did with the Bard, but I had forgotten about it. This time around, reading their charming adaptations of Shakespeare's plays generated in me an urge to embark on a similar project about a pre-Hispanic classic. Soon after, I also read Peter Ackroyd's version of *The Canterbury Tales* (2009), Arshia Sattar's adaptation of *The Ramayana* (2016), as well as Neil Gaiman's *Norse Mythology* (2017), a reimagining. Yes, that's exactly what I was after: an old text with a new voice; that is, not a translation per se but a recalibration.

I feel a particular debt to Father Francisco Ximénez de Quesada (1666–*ca.*1722), the Dominican friar, philologist, and ethnographer *avant la lettre* to whom we owe the written version of the *Popol Vuh*. Had he not devoted his energy to the rescue of this myth of creation and the epic saga of the K'iche' people, our knowledge of them today would be all the more elusive. A passionate conservationist—he learned Kaqchikel, which is closely related to K'iche' and Tz'utujil, rather quickly, around 1691—Father Ximénez lived in Chichicastenango between 1701 and 1703. (Only scattered biographical information on him is available.) There he committed his attention to listening to the Maya oral traditions. He also authored two other important works, *Historia de la provincia de San Vicente de Chiapa y Guatemala de la orden de predicadores* (History of the Province of San Vicente de Chiapa and Guatemala, 1715) and *Primera parte del tesoro de las lenguas cakchiquel, quiché y zutuhil, en que las dichas lenguas se traducen a la nuestra, española* (First Part of the Thesaurus of the Languages Cakchiquel, K'iche', and Tz'utujil, circa 1701).

Some portray Father Ximénez's effort as an appropriation. He first did a translation in two columns, with K'iche' on the left and Spanish on the right, and then he produced a prose version. His work was stored in the Convento de Santo Domingo until the Dominicans were expelled from what was called the Federación Centroamericana in 1830. Needless to say, it has become a sport to attack Spanish conquistadors and missionaries—and for good reason. Yet as Joseph Brodsky once posited in a memorable poem about Mexico, without the Europeans there would be no Latin America, for better or worse. Father Ximénez was certainly an unreliable translator. He shaped parts in a way that allowed the text to be used as a conduit for the Christian doctrine. Subsequent scholars, doing comparative work on his versions of *Popol Vuh*, have described his knowledge of K'iche' language and culture as limited, even biased.

Still, to me his effort, misguided as it might have been, is an act of courage that validates the quest of the K'iche people. How much of the story is his? In what sense is the enabler responsible for what is ultimately being enabled? Was Father Ximénez also a "reteller"? So many other hands—amanuenses, interpreters, and so on—are at work here, pushing the reader to question what is authentic and what is invention. However, in spite of the striking similarities to the Bible in the narrative, especially the books of Genesis and Exodus (the process and imagery of creation, the role of deities as scheming benefactors, reward and punishment as motifs, the importance of superhuman leaders, and so on), it is the originality, endurance, and fearlessness of the K'iche' people that shines in the pages. Tradition is as much what we inherit as what we do with it.

My predecessor in the task of retelling the *Popol Vuh* is the Mexican essayist, historian, and playwright Ermilo Abreu Gómez (1894–1971), who in 1934 wrote a groundbreaking biography of Sor Juana Inés de la Cruz. His fanciful volume *Las leyendas del Popol Vuh* (1964) is simply endearing.

My own version is infused by my lifelong devotion to Latin American literature. Indeed, I see this K'iche' almanac as a descendant of another extraordinary genealogical saga, Gabriel García Márquez's *One Hundred Years of Solitude* (1967), in which, as it happens, a set of twins also holds center stage.

My sources in this retelling have been, first and foremost, the ever-popular edition by Adrián Recinos, *Popol Vuh: Las antiguas historias del*

Quiché (1947); Victor Montejo's *Popol Vuh: A Sacred Book of the Maya* (1999); and Allen J. Christenson's *Popol Vuh: Sacred Book of the K'iche' Maya People* (2003).

I also perused Carl Scherzer's *Las historias del origen de los indios de esta provincia de Guatemala* (1857); Charles Étienne Brasseur de Bourbourg's *Popol vuh. Le livre sacré et les mythes de l'antiquité américaine, avec les livres héroïques et historiques des Quichés* (1861); Leonhard and Jena Schultze's *Popol Vuh: das heilige Buch der Quiché-Índio von Guatemala* (1944); Delia Goetz and Sylvanus G. Morley's *Popol Vuh: The Sacred Book of the Ancient Quiché Maya* (1950); Munro S. Edmonson's *The Book of Counsel: The Popol Vuh of the Quiche Maya of Guatemala* (1971); Agustín Estrada Monroy's *Popol Vuh: Empiezan las historias del origen de los índios de esta provincia de Guatemala* (1973); Dennis Tedlock's *Popol Vuh: The Mayan Book of the Dawn of Life* (1985); Sam Colop's *Popol Wuj: Versión poética K'iche'* (1999); and Michael Bazzett's *The Popol Vuh: A New Verse Translation* (2018).

For context, I frequently consulted, among other foundational texts, the work of Oswaldo Chinchilla Mazariegos, especially the magnificent *Art and Myth of the Ancient Maya* (2017).

In *A Pre-Columbian Bestiary* (2020), I offer a catalog of Aymara, Aztec, Inca, Maya, Nahua, and other indigenous beasts from Latin America, authentic and fictional. The fauna from *Popol Vuh* makes a stellar appearance.

Homero Aridjis and Betty Ferber commented on various drafts of the "retelling." *1,000 gracias por la amistad y el ojo crítico.*

My gratitude to Nathan Rostron, Jodi Marchowsky, and the extraordinary Restless Books staff. Also, Youssef Boucetta helped with copyediting and Juan Antonio Us Maldonado provided expertise on the original.

A word about the spelling of K'iche' names. There is an ongoing debate about their transliteration. Scholars take notoriously opposing views. The word "K'iche'" itself, for instance, is sometimes spelled *quiche*, *qu'iche*, *kiche*, *kiché*, and *k'iche'*, among other configurations. For the most part, I have opted to approximate, and occasionally juxtapose, the rules established by the Academia de las Lenguas Mayas in Guatemala, using apostrophes as necessary, except when a word has become part of popular knowledge.

—ILAN STAVANS

Illustrator's Note

I grew up in the Mesoamerica region, where the stories of *Popol Vuh* take place. It is a world known for its exuberant nature and its marked contrasts in its modern and ancestral societies. In my art, I portrayed the stages of the creation of human beings and nature through the use of vibrant color palettes, while using darker colors to portray Xibalba, the heartrending Maya underworld. The intimate relationship of the Maya culture with nature and animals was a great inspiration to my artwork.

The arrival of the Spanish conquistadors predestined the decline of the K'iche' society, the subjugation of their culture, and the beginning of a new era. It has been very meaningful to me to be able to lend artistic and visual language to a work that is an important piece of the Maya historical memory, mythology, and wisdom among new generations. I hope that my art helps readers immerse themselves in an infinite universe of imagination and charm. A fantastic world where human beings are made of corn, where life on earth and the underworld are intertwined between mountains and volcanoes, feathered snakes, jaguars, coyotes, wild cats, kingdoms of colorful birds, jocote trees, avocado, cocoa, mango, and apple.

—GABRIELA LARIOS

About the Authors and Illustrator

ILAN STAVANS is Professor of Humanities, Latin America and Latino Culture at Amherst College and the publisher of Restless Books. He has translated *Lazarillo de Tormes*, Sor Juana Inés de la Cruz, Jorge Luis Borges, Pablo Neruda, Mariano Azuela, and Juan Rulfo into English, Emily Dickinson and Elizabeth Bishop into Spanish, Yehuda Halevi and Yehuda Amichai from Hebrew, Isaac Bashevis Singer from Yiddish, and Shakespeare, Cervantes, and *The Little Prince* into Spanglish. His books include *On Borrowed Words, Dictionary Days, Quixote, On Self-Translation,* and *The Wall.* He edited the *Oxford Book of Jewish Stories*, the *Norton Anthology of Latino Literature*, and *Becoming Americans: Four Centuries of Immigrant Writing*. The recipient of numerous awards and honors, his work, rendered into twenty languages, has been adapted for film, TV, radio, and theater.

Internationally renowned poet, novelist, diplomat, and environmental activist HOMERO ARIDJIS is the author of *Eyes to See Otherwise, 1492: The Life and Times of Juan Cabezón of Castile*, and *News of the Earth*, among many other books. He has been president of PEN International and Mexico's ambassador to UNESCO. He has championed an appreciation of indigenous cultures as well as environmental awareness worldwide.

London-based Salvadoran artist and illustrator GABRIELA LARIOS received her Master of Arts from Camberwell College of Arts, UK in 2007 thanks to an Alban Scholarship. She creates whimsical and colorful collage illustrations that celebrate her deep love of children's books, textiles, and folk art. Her creative world derives from her interest in storytelling and the natural world. Her work has been exhibited in London, Europe, and abroad and has appeared in various international books and magazines.

RESTLESS BOOKS is an independent, nonprofit publisher devoted to championing essential voices from around the world whose stories speak to us across linguistic and cultural borders. We seek extraordinary international literature for adults and young readers that feeds our restlessness: our hunger for new perspectives, passion for other cultures and languages, and eagerness to explore beyond the confines of the familiar.

Through cultural programming, we aim to celebrate immigrant writing and bring literature to underserved communities. We believe that immigrant stories are a vital component of our cultural consciousness; they help to ensure awareness of our communities, build empathy for our neighbors, and strengthen our democracy.

Visit us at www.restlessbooks.org